THE ROWAN

Severn House Titles by Davis Bunn

PRIME DIRECTIVE
ISLAND OF TIME
FORBIDDEN

THE ROWAN

Davis Bunn

**SEVERN
HOUSE**

First world edition published in Great Britain and the USA in 2023
by Severn House, an imprint of Canongate Books Ltd,
14 High Street, Edinburgh EH1 1TE.

severnhouse.com

British Library Cataloguing-in-Publication Data
A CIP catalogue record for this title is available from the British Library.

ISBN-13: 978-1-4483-1112-5 (cased)
ISBN-13: 978-1-4483-1113-2 (e-book)

All Severn House titles are printed on acid-free paper.

MIX
Paper from
responsible sources
FSC® C013056

Typeset by Palimpsest Book Production Ltd., Falkirk, Stirlingshire, Scotland.
Printed and bound in Great Britain by TJ Books, Padstow, Cornwall.

Praise for Davis Bunn

"I absolutely loved this story! *The Rowan* is a powerful
political thriller that delves both into sci-fi and fantasy.
The result is a mesmerizing page-turner"
David Lipman, producer of the *Ironman* and *Shrek* films,
on *The Rowan*

"I was not prepared for this. It's somewhere between
spectacular and astonishingly compelling. Bunn's writing has
never been stronger. After I finished, I could not let it go"
Phyllis Tickle, Senior Contributing Editor, *Publishers Weekly*,
on *Island of Time*

"A wild ride"
Kirkus Reviews on *Island of Time*

"A fast-paced, retro-feeling sci-fy mystery. Bunn offers readers
a sure guide through his far-future setting . . . A pleasure. This
is good fun"
Publishers Weekly on *Prime Directive*

"The emotional power demonstrates Bunn's extraordinary gift of
story-telling, and solidifies his place as one of the great writers
of a generation"
Charles Martin, *NYT* bestselling author of
The Mountain Between Us, on *Firefly Cove*

"Bunn's imaginative thriller combines propulsive plotting with
sharp observations"
Publishers Weekly on *Burden of Proof*

"A stylistically complex work that lends itself to a variety
of audiences"
Library Journal Starred Review of *The Domino Effect*

About the author

Davis Bunn's novels have sold in excess of eight million copies in twenty-six languages. He has appeared on numerous national bestseller lists, and his novels have been Main or Featured Selections with every major US bookclub. Recent titles have been named Best Book of the Year by both *Library Journal* and *Suspense Magazine*, as well as earning Top Pick and starred reviews from *Publishers Weekly*, *RT Reviews*, *Kirkus*, and *Booklist*. Currently Davis serves as Writer-In-Residence at Regent's Park College, Oxford University. He speaks around the world on aspects of creative writing. Davis also publishes under the pseudonym of Thomas Locke.

This book is dedicated to:
Frank and Gretchen Ceverney

With heartfelt thanks for the wonderfully creative gift of
their haven by the sea.

PROLOGUE

The backpacker in front of Val walked down the ferry's gangplank, gave the harbor city one look, and said, 'OK, I've seen enough.'

'Nobody does grim like the Russians,' Val agreed.

The woman's name was Arbila, mother Spanish, father Dutch. She was mid-twenties, very beautiful with a sexy, crushed-rose manner. Arbila had spent the four-hour journey from Hokkaido toking on joints offered by fellow travelers who clearly hoped to hook up. Male and female alike. On their approach to the Russian port city of Korsakov, a very stoned Arbila had sought protection in the form of Val. 'I don't see why we had to spend all this time going in circles.'

A good-looking Black guy named Bernard was stationed at the foot of the walkway. He smiled at Arbila's approach, took in the long legs and cut-offs and boots and unsteady walk, and offered her an envelope. 'Russian city, Russian rules.'

'What's this?'

Val accepted envelopes for them both and pulled Arbila away. 'He told us on the boat. Twice. Money for a day visa. And we need to spend some rubles.'

'I don't want anything from this place except the exit.'

Val steered the woman across the empty concrete plaza. A massive statue of Lenin pointed in the direction they had come, which Val thought was fairly typical for Russia's manner of welcome. Customs occupied the front segment of a warehouse-type structure. A bored officer took their payments, stamped their passports, ignored their packs, and waved them through.

'I still don't get why that guy on the boat handed us money,' Arbila said. 'He's after something. Got to be.'

'Bernard said he's part of a volunteer organization. People who've made this trip before. Those who can, help.'

'I don't buy it. Do you buy it?' Arbila's slurred voice echoed around the almost-empty chamber. 'I'm telling you, he wants what they all want.'

Three heavyset women in headkerchiefs and stolid expressions stood behind an Intourist cafe counter. Val settled Arbila in a line of uncomfortable plastic chairs, dumped her own pack on the next seat, then asked the same question she had posed a dozen times already. More. 'Why are you making this trip?'

'Same as you.' Without the need to vamp for her entourage, Arbila looked smaller. Sadder. Exposed. 'The birds.'

'We both know that's not true.'

'What do you want me to say?' Arbila took a two-armed hold on her pack, hugging it like a stuffed animal. 'Soon as I heard about this, I had to come. The draw.'

The draw. Val had heard the words any number of times. Ever since entering the Hokkaido port guesthouse, meeting others waiting for the unreliable Russian ferry. *The draw.* The other travelers used it as a call sign.

When Val realized she was not getting anything more, she went in search of tea.

Though Val was only the fifth customer in line, she waited almost twenty minutes to be served. Clearly Russia's drive to overhaul the sullen Soviet attitude toward customer service had not made it this far east. The remaining rubles covered two teas and a pair of cheese rolls Val would not dream of eating. When she arrived back, Arbila had settled onto the concrete floor, pack for a pillow, coat for her mattress, deep in a stoner's snooze. A trio of young men hovered by the rear windows like a pack of scruffy curs.

Val noticed how their unofficial tour guide was watching her, and decided now was her chance for some semi-private questions and maybe a few answers. She set one tea and both rolls on the floor beside Arbila, hefted her pack, and headed back outside.

As she approached the rear doors, a crowd of new arrivals surged through Customs, chattering happily, excited and fresh despite their rumpled state. Val slowed and listened as the rainbow assortment of races and languages passed. She gathered they had just arrived on the island chain's only official tour package – flight to Moscow, another five hours in the air to this province's main airport, then a bus to the harbor. She counted twenty-seven in that group. Older than most of the ferry passengers. Their trek gear was better quality, their packs mostly new.

Val stepped outdoors, peeled the lid off her tea, sipped, and breathed the salt-laden air. July on Sakhalin Island had her standing in a pewter realm. The sky was veiled, but the sunlight was still strong enough to cast the world in shades of silver-grey. Sky, sea, empty harbor-front, all the same shadowless gleam.

These were the moments Val lived for.

Each new investigation had a brief time, sometimes an hour, occasionally long as a week, when Val felt more than just fully alive. She was as happy as she had ever known. Totally free of the past and the future both. She felt like that now. Standing on the verge of another fresh discovery, feeling the electric high of something big. Leading to a story she would write better than anyone else on Earth.

She heard the door creak open and did not turn around. The handsome Black man stepped up and said, 'You're the journalist.'

'And you are Bernard Severant. Formerly of Martinique. Doing postdoc research in microbiology at University College London. Until you signed on as unofficial tour guide, handing out rubles to people you've never met before.'

'Impressive.'

'The woman who guided us from the Hokkaido guesthouse to the ferry told the travelers to watch out for you. I listened.' Val faced him. 'That's what I do. Listen.'

He had a quiet manner and a gentle smile. And a lovely accent. British and French both. 'I imagine you are excellent at asking questions as well.'

'Want to find out for yourself?'

He waved one hand in silent invitation.

'Here's what I see. Sixty-one people from over a dozen countries make their way to Hakodate, the northernmost port in Japan. They fill the cheap guesthouses. They take the ferry that runs twice each week through the summer, the only boat making regular runs from Japan to Russia. There doesn't need to be more. There were a few local merchants on board, otherwise the boat was ours. What's more, the ferry doesn't operate to any schedule they've bothered to translate. Which made the lady who popped into all the guesthouses very important indeed. So we travel to this lovely destination, where we're greeted by a guy who offers us money. Like all this was part of some great secret plan.'

Bernard waited, then, 'Is there a question?'

'Tell me what I'm missing. How's that for a start?'

'You neglected to mention the new arrivals from Moscow.'

'I didn't need to.'

'And you know what happens next.'

'I'm assuming everybody clambers on board the next boat to the Kurils.'

'Kunashir Island. Correct.'

'OK, Bernard. So let's start with why here, and why now? What draws this crowd from all over the globe?' She waved her hand at Lenin's statue, and the otherwise empty quay. 'Nobody in their right mind would call this a tourist destination.'

'But this is, as you say, merely a way station.'

'Same question, Bernard. Why are we here?'

He nodded. 'May I ask your name?'

'Valentina Garnier. I go by Val.'

'You are French?'

'My father was French Canadian.'

'And your mother?'

'American. Louisiana Creole.'

He switched to French. 'You speak the tongue?'

'Badly. Answer the question, Bernard.'

'Such an excellent question certainly deserves an answer.' He pointed to where a derelict ferry was pulling up to the harbor wall. 'The answer, Valentina, lies just four hours away. And we will depart as soon as our last remaining group arrives . . . And here they come now.'

A military truck and an unmarked black sedan pulled up by the boundary fence. The sedan beeped its horn. Again. A uniformed customs agent scurried out, saluted, and opened the gate. The two vehicles drove across the concrete plaza and halted by the ferry's gangplank. Val watched as eleven soldiers and three dark-suited men walked on board.

Three minutes later, the ferry's whistle blasted a long note.

Val shouldered her pack. 'Are we in danger?'

'Every day on this Earth carries a certain risk, no?' If Bernard was troubled by the official Russian presence, he did not show it. 'What this is, Valentina, is inevitable.'

ONE

Six days earlier

Three o'clock on a cloudless July afternoon, Val Garnier sat on her balcony nursing a hangover. Her apartment was on the top floor of a renovated federalist warehouse on Charles Street, midway between the Maryland State House and the Annapolis waterfront. Tourists passed along the cobblestone street in chattering clutches, their footsteps chiming like leather rain.

A black SUV was parked on the side street, half hidden in shadows, tinted windows masking the occupants from passersby. She had noticed it while spinning the Peloton bike stationed by her bedroom window. It was still there, over two hours later. There were any number of reasons why such a vehicle could be parked three and a half blocks from the state capitol. It was probably nothing more than boredom and ego that had Val's senses sniffing at a possible story, as in, why somebody with enough clout to order her checked out would be interested. The thing was, this had happened before. Twice. When a major figure became aware of her digging into items the power structure wanted to stay hidden.

Today, however, there was a difference.

She had submitted her last story four months ago. Since then, she had been on a lecture tour, promoting her latest book. Which was about a different story, one that had broken almost two years back.

All of which suggested she was not the reason why the blank-faced federal-type vehicle was parked there, nose out. Silent. For over two hours.

But still.

Days between assignments were bound by rules. Never let a hangover keep her from the daily workout. Never check the news until she was fully restored from the last project. Never regret all the failed moves that littered her personal history.

Never take a drink or a toke before five.

That path led to the downward spiral and the big black door. Val should know. Her mother had willfully slithered down that route after her father was lost to the cancer. Her mother, a Louisiana socialite to her last dying breath, always insisted on adding an article before naming her husband's illness. *The* cancer had ruined her existence. *The* cancer had wrecked her hopes for a brighter tomorrow. Not some generic disease endured by millions. To her, it was both specific and personal. After Val's father was laid to rest, her mother spent eight determined months meandering through an alcoholic fog until she could join him. Until finally *the* cancer indirectly ended her life as well.

Val rarely allowed herself to dwell on the past. But she was bored and restless both. Four months since her last writing project was submitted, three weeks since the book tour ended, and she itched inside her own skin. Empty hours like this carried risks. They drew her back to bad memories, old regrets, wrong moves . . .

Wrong men.

She rose and entered the apartment, defeated by the past. On the precipice of losing her way. Again.

She was twenty-nine and felt a hundred and ten.

Val crossed to the kitchen, opened the cabinet, and pulled out the box of carved African mango-wood. She loved opening the lid, loved the wood's spicy-sweet fragrance, loved the anticipation of rolling a joint and taking that first hit. Not to mention the silver cocaine-holder, the size and shape of a lipstick tube. An unintended gift from a former so-called lover who had entered rehab. Or the little jeweled box that held her collection of pills, stolen from the bedroom of a truly bad man, for those nights when she wanted to feel very, very small, or very, very tall, or sometimes just feel nothing at all.

She loved it all far too much.

Val was almost sorry when her phone rang. She stood there a moment, phone in one hand, the other still inside the box. Then she checked the screen. She instantly felt the tight electric thrill when she saw who was calling. 'Carlton Riffkind. Can it truly be you?'

'If a reporter has me on speed-dial, I know I must be slipping.'

'Why didn't you have one of your thirty-odd minions place the call, make me wait half an hour for the big man himself?'

'Not so big. Not anymore. How are you, Val?'

Because it was Carlton who asked, she gave him an honest response. 'Between assignments. Months since I wrote a word. Bored. Scared the world has moved on without me.'

'No chance of that.'

'How are things down in the big city?'

'Oh, I still manage to make the rent. Listen, I'm holding up one end of an almost empty bar down at the Yacht Club. It's lonely here, Val. Very lonely.'

Her heart rate edged up a notch. 'The big man himself came to Annapolis?'

'Just happened to be down this way. Thought I'd stop by, see how my favorite lady was faring.'

'When was the last time you left DC?'

'Years. Longer. I can't hardly believe it myself. This far from the action, I tend to break out in hives.' Carlton had a rich way of speaking, like he was about ready to share the world's greatest secret. Or break out laughing. Or both. 'Only cure is a steady dose of single malt. I'd pay good money for some company.'

She closed the box. 'Give me twenty minutes to shower and dress. I'll be right down.'

The Annapolis Yacht Club was located at the tip of Compromise Street, a glass-fronted edifice to money and power and floating extravagance. If a K Street mover and shaker could feel at home anywhere in low-key Annapolis, it was here.

K Street was both an address and a title, applied to the most powerful of Washington lobbyists. This half-dozen or so blocks represented the underbelly of politics, and as a result had run up its share of nicknames over the years. Evil Empire was the current favorite, though a number of senators preferred Heart of Darkness. Val had mixed feelings about the people who claimed K Street residency. Most were feral beasts hunting their next million-dollar meal. What soul they had once possessed had long since been sold to whichever national government or industry group could afford their hourly rates.

Carlton Riffkind was a beast of a different stripe. Sort of.

The firm still bearing his name employed more than its share of spineless parasites. But Carlton had not been part of that group for almost a decade.

When Carlton hit fifty-five, at the top of his game, he resigned. Walked away. And hung up a new shingle on the quietly residential M Street in Georgetown. Nineteen blocks and a world removed from power central. Close enough to his federalist townhouse for Carlton to walk.

The K Street pack sneered over Carlton's transition to what they assumed was a semi-retired guy's slide into anonymity. After all, Carlton's most recent presidential candidate had suffered a massive defeat. The competition assumed Carlton's time was over. He had made his dime and was taking a slow limo cruise to easy street. Goodbye and good riddance.

Val knew differently.

A very rare sort of individual walked the Washington shadows. One so singular most people pretended they did not exist.

These extraordinary predators hearkened back to the days of regional bosses and their iron grip on local unions, federal and state jobs, and voting blocks. They had no name. They needed none. They preferred not to be known at all. Their influence rested in going unseen. They were the true ghosts of Washington power.

There were never more than two or three at any time. Able to drift through administrations of both parties. Handling the uncommonly difficult and perplexing issues. Very hush-hush. Never taking credit. There and gone in the puff of cinders and softly drifting smoke.

Incredibly expensive.

Another dark-windowed SUV was parked in the yacht club's forecourt, this one a Lincoln Navigator. As she passed, she slipped her phone from her pocket and shot three quick photos of the license plate.

She entered the club and used the empty foyer to send the pics to her fastest and best online snoop. Requested an ID of the owner.

Old habits.

When she entered the upstairs bar, a burly guy in a federal-agent type navy suit and club tie stepped from the corner shadows, checked her out, and announced, 'Mr Riffkind, your guest has arrived.'

'My favorite lady, right on time.' Carlton Riffkind rose from his corner stool, walked over, bussed both cheeks European-style. The man was nothing if not debonair. 'You're looking marvelous, Val. More lovely than I recall.'

'I'm bored out of my tiny mind.'

'Then the slow hours definitely agree with you.'

'Liar.'

'Now that is one thing I have never done. To you, at least.' He led her back toward the open French doors. 'Would the lady like a table?'

'I've always enjoyed a front-row seat.'

'A stool at the bar it is.' He pointed to the bartender holding a bottle of vintage Margaux. 'I seem to remember you preferred grapes of the red variety.'

She nodded approval at the label. 'I don't know why I'm here, but your windup certainly wins points.'

'All the time you and I have spent together . . .'

'Not so much. A few hours here and there.'

'I've never had the opportunity to know who you are. Which is a true shame.'

She leaned back. Inspecting the man who billed his hours at five figures. 'Where are you going with this?'

He pretended at surprise. 'What, an older gentleman isn't permitted to ask a personal question or two?'

She watched the bartender open the bottle. Decided anyone willing to pay two hundred dollars for a vintage Bordeaux could call the shots. 'Ask away.'

'How does one become a features writer? This day and age, it'd seem almost impossible. Be the first with a story no one else has discovered. Take weeks to investigate—'

'Longer.'

'Months, then. You've always impressed me, Val. I'm interested in knowing how you got your start.'

She watched the bartender slowly decant the bottle. Dribbling the ruby liquid down the side of the crystal vase, letting the fifteen-year-old wine aerate. 'You know I was orphaned.'

'I believe I heard that somewhere.'

Val thought he was being overly casual. But it was hard to tell with a man like Carlton, who had spent a lifetime showing the world the face they wanted to see. 'When I was a kid, nobody wanted to talk about what happened. Anytime I walked into a room, people went totally quiet. Almost guilty. Which basically told me they had been talking about my late parents. Especially my mother.'

She stopped then. The bartender was taking overlong to empty the bottle, which probably meant he was paying too much attention to what she was saying. Val waited while he splashed a bit into the oversized goblet and handed it over. She went through the sniff-and-swill-and-swallow routine. Which, in this case, was an absolute delight. She toasted Carlton and said, 'Wow.'

'You are most welcome.'

Val remained silent as the waiter filled her glass to the proper spot, then retreated. Only then did she ask, 'Where was I?'

'Adults being adults.'

'You know the Field School.'

'The private high school over by Glover Park. Of course I know it. Several of their administrators are driving Cadillacs my friends and relatives have personally financed.'

'They have a scholarship program.'

'Now that I didn't know.'

'It's not public knowledge. At fifty thou a year tuition, they'd be deluged with requests. Anyway, I was looking for a way out, and one of my teachers told me I should apply. So I wrote up my personal story as an investigation. Started with my father's death from pulmonary cancer. Then my mother plying the drink and the pills until she followed him eight months later. And used that as a basis for a story on sadness and loss and the voluntary suicides that go unnoticed.'

He started nodding in time to her words. 'I remember something about that. The *Post* did it.'

'My first byline.'

'How old were you?'

'Eleven when I wrote it. Twelve when it came out.'

He laughed, shook his head, and toasted her with his glass. 'A late bloomer.'

She lifted her glass. 'Same question, Carlton. Why are we here?'

But Carlton showed no desire to proceed. If anything, he pulled back. Turned into the inscrutable political Sphinx. Ordered another whisky. Commented on a passing yacht. Said something about her wine.

All the while, they had the entire bar to themselves. Beautiful July afternoon, utterly pristine conditions, blue sky and sparkling waters and just enough wind to keep the temperature comfy. Normally the crowd would be massed around every table, the conversation loud and well lubricated. Their only companion was the lone dark-suited security, who barely separated himself from the shadows.

Finally Val took hold of the controls. 'I like you, Carlton. I know, it's a dangerous thing to say. But you've always been straight with me. So I'm going to return the favor. I am signing up. You've helped me establish the foundations to two stories, and they have both turned out to be real winners. So whatever it is that's brought you up here, you don't have to pitch me. I mean, sure, the wine is a fabulous touch. But it's overkill. You need me to do something. Pursue another story. One that by the looks of things is highly sensitive. And I'm telling you, I'm your girl. Just point me in—'

'The vice president's daughter is missing.'

She breathed around this and the torrent of sudden questions. And waited.

'You know about her?'

'The bare bones, sure.' It had been hard to miss some of the stories, even when Val was on the other side of the world. Such as when Lauren Dale and the star of Washington's basketball team were caught dancing in the Mall's pool. Drunk, drugged, nearly naked. The night before the Wizards were due for game six of the divisional play-offs.

'Lauren Dale, twenty-four years old, in trouble almost constantly for the past nine. Three months ago, she slips away from her security detail. Again. And runs away. Again. Her moves were hard to track at first, because she'd managed to obtain a fake passport from one of her low-class pals. So off she goes.' He glanced over. 'To Russia.'

'Get out of town.'

'Place called Sakhalin Island. Ever heard of it?'

'I don't . . . Somewhere.'

'Russia's easternmost province. North of Japan. Beyond Sakhalin lies the Kuril Islands, which Russia and Japan have been arguing over for seventy years. Not what you would call a five-star garden spot. And that was her destination. Kunashir Island, the southern tip of the Kuril Island chain, about twenty miles north of Japan's Hokkaido.'

'I don't get it.'

'On that point, you and I certainly agree.' A sip of whisky, then, 'Lauren Dale considers it a hardship to stay overnight someplace without room service. But this island has no, repeat, no, hotel. Not even a guesthouse. Lauren takes the only tour service operating on the island.'

'Where does she stay?'

'Good question. The tours run out of Moscow. They go once a week and just during the nine or ten weeks of high summer. Normally the only people who make the trip are birdwatchers. Serious types. They ferry over, then hike north, away from the Russian military compounds that ring the southern perimeter. Guarding against another Japanese invasion.'

'Wait. Lauren camped?'

'Pretty much had to. The place doesn't even have roads. A lot of hot springs and nesting birds. Nothing else. Nada.'

Val tried her best to track ahead, but could only come up with, 'She's gone there to straighten out? Some secret Russian hot spring miracle cure?'

'My first thought. And the answer is, nobody knows.' Another sip. 'Will you go check this out?'

'Didn't you hear what I said? Yes, Carlton. I'm in. Definitely. One question, though. Who's paying?'

'A lady after my own heart. The answer is, as far as you're concerned it's me and me alone.' He reached into his jacket, came out with a bulky envelope. 'A personal debit card in your name. Holds thirty thousand dollars.'

This was new. 'What's the catch? I mean, I go and you officially own the story, tell me what I can and can't print?'

He tapped the envelope with his glass. 'This includes a certified statement, declaring you own all rights. What you write, all photos, the works. With one caveat. Unofficially you'll be traveling on the federal dime, Val. Keep careful records of where this money goes.'

'I can live with that.'

'I'd like you to leave tomorrow.'

'That's pushing it.' She saw him readying the arguments and said, 'Carlton, you're the payer. If speed is that important—'

'It is. We think. Everything about this carries a flashing red alert.'

'Then tomorrow it is.' She tucked the envelope in her purse, then signaled the bartender. When he approached, she said, 'I need you to put the rest of this fabulous wine back in the bottle. The Margaux is going to help me pack.'

TWO

Carlton Riffkind didn't really feel the three whiskies until he left the yacht club ten minutes after Val. He crossed the parking lot and walked along the quayside, past all the fancy boats sparkling in the sunlight. His footsteps were unsteady and there was nothing he could do about it. It wasn't the Scotch so much as age, and that troubled him, how the years had managed to creep up and bring him to a point where three glasses could partially disconnect his mind from his legs. There had once been a time when half a bottle wouldn't faze him. He smiled as he passed a trio of young lovelies, who did their practiced best pretending he did not exist. Which was good for a melancholy sigh.

The security agent who had accompanied him upstairs rose from the SUV's front passenger seat and opened the rear door. As Carlton slipped inside, he noticed that the three ladies had stopped and turned around and were now watching. Which was good for a secret chuckle. Not even age could tarnish the lure of power.

The woman seated beside him slapped her laptop shut and asked, 'Did she buy it?'

'Hook, line, and sinker.'

'We could be making a dreadful mistake. I just watched her cross the lot in what could only be described as a drunken stroll.'

'Impossible. She only had a glass and a half.'

'Then she was dosed on something else. Grey?'

The agent up front said, 'The lady was too stoned to stand upright.'

Carlton shook his head. 'It has to be a ploy.'

'Why would she do that?'

'I have no idea. But I'm telling you, she was nearer to sobriety than I am.'

The woman reached into her shoulder bag and pulled out a manila folder bearing the diagonal red Top Secret stripe. 'This lady of yours has been in and out of trouble since she started walking.'

The flash of irritation was exactly what he needed to draw the day back into focus. 'Let's review how you and I happen to be sitting here. We need a total outsider with strong investigative powers who also happens to fit a very specific profile.'

'Other than the fact that Valentina Garnier can write, there's not a lot separating her from the VP's in-house bad girl.' Agnes Pendalon was a small, precise woman with a permanently irritated air. Her steel-gray hair was pulled back into a bun so tight it stretched the skin of her face and turned her eyes to slits. Or so Carlton had always thought. She surveyed the world like an angry bird. One glance of her venomous disdain was enough to deflate any stuffed Washington ego. 'There are a lot of writers out there, Carlton.'

'How many have won a Pulitzer before they turned thirty?'

'That was then and this is now. I'm telling you, the young lady just staggered away from your meeting.'

'She was totally wasted,' Grey agreed. 'Almost didn't make it across the street. Came within inches of being flattened by a delivery van.'

'Which begs the question, should we find another option . . .' Agnes was halted by Grey's phone chiming.

He frowned over the incoming message, then swiveled in his seat, holding it up for her to inspect. 'Homeland reports a hit on our vehicle's license plate.'

Carlton resisted a sudden urge to laugh out loud.

The agent's phone chimed a second time. He checked the readout, said, 'They traced the query to a Singapore IP. Have to assume it's a cut-out.'

Agnes noticed Carlton's smile. 'This doesn't mean—'

'Hold that thought.' He pointed out her side window. 'Heads up. Here she comes now.'

'What?' Agnes spun around. 'I can't—'

'Run? I absolutely agree.' Carlton wiggled one finger. 'Roll down your window, why don't you. Tell the lady hello.'

There was no hint of drugs or wine to Val's gait. She almost skipped across the parking lot and smiled brightly as the window came down. 'Carlton, I'm so glad I managed to catch you before . . . Oh, hi there.'

Swift as a starling's flight, Val lifted the phone from her purse and snapped the woman's photograph.

Agnes leaned back, trying to remove herself from view. 'Grey.'

The big agent opened his door and rose to full height while Val shot his picture as well. Grey reached out and said, 'Give.'

'Here's the thing. I'm linked to auto-store in the cloud. I'm also auto-forwarding to my pal in Singapore. I guess you've already caught wind of that cut-out, right?' When Grey started forward, Val lifted her hand and sped up her words. But she held her ground. 'If your man unlawfully steals my device, all this goes viral. That's including our chat in the bar, Carlton.'

Carlton said, 'Call off your agent.'

Agnes sighed the words. 'Grey, stand down.'

'Yeah, Grey. Good dog.'

'Grey, open the door. Agnes, make room for the lady of the hour.' Carlton swung around and took the fold-down seat behind the driver. When Val slipped inside and Grey closed the rear door, Carlton asked, 'What do you want, Val?'

'Why don't we start with names.'

When Agnes remained silent, still, fuming, Carlton said, 'She has your picture. She'll have your name soon enough.'

Agnes made do with a tight nod, a glare.

'Agnes Pendalon. CIA's deputy chief of operations.'

'Grey I've already met. And the driver I don't need to know.' Val smiled brightly. 'Is the CIA your client, Carlton?'

'Hardly. I'm working for the vice president.'

'So why doesn't somebody give me the other half.'

Another nod from the woman, and Carlton said, 'There are two parts. First, the VP's daughter. It's not as simple as I made it out to be.'

'She only needs to hear that part, Carlton.'

'Actually, ma'am, I need it all. Go on, Carlton. The daughter.'

'She's not actually missing.'

THREE

Carlton went on, 'Lauren Dale only remained in Russia six days.'

'Not long for a cure.'

'Wait, it gets better. She traveled with a federal agent by the name of Jadyn James. No previous connection to the family.'

'How did they hook up?'

'Apparently Jadyn was friends with the daughter's one confidante among the VP's security detail. She alerted Jadyn, who . . .'

'What?'

'This is where things get weird,' Carlton warned.

Agnes snorted. 'This entire episode defines absurd.'

'Weirder, then. Jadyn had already decided to take the same trip. With his entire family.'

Val leaned back. Frowned at the side window.

'At first, all the VP's family knew was Lauren had slipped away again. But Jadyn had left a confidential note with his boss—'

'Who was on vacation at the time,' Agnes said. 'And didn't see the memo until four days after the daughter's disappearance.'

Val asked Agnes, 'How is the CIA involved in all this?'

'How do you think?' Agnes went on, 'Soon as we learned Lauren went to Russia, we sent two agents to track her down. Traveling as civilians, seeing as how currently our relations with Russia are tricky.'

Carlton continued, 'So they get to the Sakhalin harbor town, the only place with a sometime ferry service to the island. And guess who's there to greet them.'

'Lauren?'

Carlton nodded. 'None other. With the James family.'

'I don't get it.'

'Nobody does.'

'Lauren Dale goes to Russia. To watch birds, take a cure, something. Six days later, she and her agent pal and his family are all back at the port, ready to greet her hunters.'

'Flies home,' Carlton continued. 'Greets her family. Apologizes for making a fuss. She stays for a month. Plays the perfect daughter.

No scandal, no drinking, no drugs they could find. Then she takes off again. This time to Nova Scotia. Another mystery destination for someone who feeds on the wild city life.' Carlton gave the CIA director a chance to break in. When Agnes remained silent, he went on, 'Lauren warned her folks if they came after her, she would disappear for good.'

'So you want me to go to Nova Scotia, check out her commune.'

'No commune. Nothing hinky that we have been able to uncover. She's enrolled in the university. Graduate studies in oceanography and statistical analysis of related experimentation.'

'So what . . .'

'There are others. A wife here. Husband there. Couple of sons. They've all taken the same trip. Most have come back. Not all.'

Agnes snapped, 'That's enough.'

'She should know,' Carlton replied.

'Not until we decide.'

'OK, Agnes. Decide. Because she can't go without knowing. I won't allow it.' He took the woman's tight glare as the only accord he was going to get. 'We know of two congressional aides who have also made the trip. Possibly some scientists. We're checking.'

Val's words emerged very slowly. 'To an island in Russia.'

'Right.'

She addressed Agnes. 'You've sent others. I know you have.'

'Two sets of professionals,' Carlton replied. 'One team from the Agency, another private.'

'And?'

'They say it's nothing. A beautiful, untouched Siberian-style wilderness. Great wildlife. One of the most relaxing times they've ever had. We're getting the exact same response from everyone.'

'A vacation. That's it.'

'The best they've ever had.'

'I need to put off my trip one more day,' Val said.

'Timing is crucial, Val.'

'Maybe so. But first I need to speak with the agent who went out with the VP's daughter.'

'Jadyn James,' Agnes said. 'I can make that happen.'

'Not at Langley, please. Or the White House. Someplace neutral.'

'Understood.'

Carlton asked, 'You're still up for this?'

Val's response was to ask Agnes, 'I'm still not clear on why this so concerns the clandestine services they'd send out a big gun like yourself.'

When Agnes showed no interest in replying, Carlton said, 'We had no idea this was happening. Then I'm informed about the VP's daughter. I look into it. Two of my allies at the Agency help. We discover a number of other people have made the same—'

'We *think* they've gone. We have no clear evidence.'

'We know,' Carlton insisted. 'The peripheral evidence is too glaring.' To Val, 'A number of scientists. We're also fairly certain about a congresswoman and several aides—'

'Enough,' Agnes snapped.

'—And her family,' Carlton finished.

'This has the makings of a major story,' Val said, watching Agnes. 'With or without understanding everything.'

'Some questions are outside your boundaries,' Agnes snapped.

Val smiled. 'We'll see.'

When Pendalon merely smoldered, Carlton said, 'Like I said, there's just the one tour service with officially sanctioned trips. They're sold out for the next twenty-one months. Your best bet is to follow the backpacker's route.'

'Fly to Tokyo, connect to Hokkaido. Ferry to Russia. Second ferry to the bird-infested island. Got it.'

'You need to send us regular reports,' Agnes said. 'We're after clarity. Daily reports. Hourly.'

'Long as the story remains mine, and timing of its release to the public is my decision.'

Agnes shook her head. 'We have no repeat no interest in this going public until we have a firm grasp on what is going on here.'

Val did not raise her voice. She didn't need to. 'Timing of my article's release is my decision.'

Carlton said, 'I've already supplied Val with a notarized document confirming her full ownership and control of everything she uncovers.'

Agnes protested, 'I didn't authorize anything of the sort.'

Carlton replied, 'Just the same, that's how it has to be.'

Her features tightened into one pale knot. But she remained silent.

Val opened her door, slipped out. 'This has been great, really. See you tomorrow.'

Agnes glared at the young woman's departure, then noticed Carlton's expression. 'Oh, stop looking so smug.'

FOUR

The interview of Jadyn James was set for eleven o'clock. Carlton even sprang for a limo, which said a lot about the guy. Val spent the ninety-minute ride into DC going through the notes she'd made the previous evening. There was a series of gaps to what she had been told. The mystery they had not revealed stayed just out of reach. Neither good nor bad. But powerful. Like an unknown spice.

At this stage of any new investigation, it all came down to what Val did not know. What the initial sources left out. What they did not want her discovering. Val was mostly OK with that. Putting together a solid piece usually came down to finding the rocks they didn't want her to uncover.

As they crossed the GW Bridge, Val turned to a fresh page and began sketching the unseen questions. She wasn't after clarity. Not just yet. First and foremost, she needed to start giving voice to the hidden.

Starting with the question that drifted in the limo's A/C like burnt cordite.

Why was the tight-faced woman involved?

On the surface, a couple of her agents went to Russia and came back . . . What? Calm? That scares a CIA director enough to go outside the Agency for an investigative journalist?

Puh-leese.

Agnes Pendalon had an immense amount of power at her disposal. The woman's narrow expression, the gunmetal glint to her eyes, the terse manner of speech, all shouted one thing. She had watched people under her command go down.

Val wrote the woman's name. Agnes Pendalon. Then the one word. *Why?* Underlined it five times.

She started to write a second question, then decided she didn't want to give it room on the page. If she did, the words would probably invade her sleep.

The question was if the danger was big enough to involve Agnes Pendalon, how was Val going to keep herself alive?

FIVE

The limo dropped Val at the Residence Inn on M Street. It was the sort of clean and faceless hotel found in any affluent city. The clientele were mostly families on a budget and white-collar corporate types. As far as Val was concerned, the place was perfect.

The limo driver must have texted an alert, because as Val entered the front doors Carlton emerged from the elevator. He nodded to the hotel receptionist and ushered her inside the lift. 'Good trip?'

'Fine. Thanks for the ride.'

He pressed the top-floor button. 'OK, you'll meet the team, then it's your show.'

'Team?'

'Agnes sent a crew.' He rocked back and forth, toes to heels. 'Little good it will do anybody. If we could find answers this way, I'd be missing the pleasure of your company.'

'Sorry, Carlton. I don't follow.'

He did not respond. The doors opened, he led her down the corridor to the last door on the right. Knocked. Used a key. Opened. 'Coffee?'

'I'm good, thanks.'

The bed and other furniture were crammed into the corner by the bathroom, making room for a long table and three office chairs and a series of laptops and cables and instruments she did not recognize. A man and a woman looked up, then went back to monitoring their equipment. Carlton asked, 'Any change?'

'James is still standing by the window. The man might as well be petrified.' The woman sipped from a mug, grimaced. 'This is the worst coffee I have ever, in my entire life, not drunk.'

'Starbucks is across the street,' the man offered. He was overweight and nearly bald, short-sleeve white shirt with a plastic pocket protector, black square glasses, tie that was probably a clip on. Total aging geek. 'I'll buy if you'll go.'

'Nobody's going anywhere,' Carlton said. 'The lady here hasn't come all this way for you to do a vanishing act.'

'Wasted trip, if you ask me.' The woman.

The man offered Val an earpiece. 'Don't worry about talking loud or anything. The room is wired.' He waited as she fitted it in her ear. 'You hear me OK?'

'Yes.' To her surprise, Carlton then started back towards the door. 'Hang on a second. You can't expect me to go in there blind. What makes this guy special? Other than the fact that he's gone on a birdwatching trip to Russia.'

'Him and his entire family.' The woman again.

Carlton said, 'We have no idea what is going on here. None.' He pointed to the man on the largest monitor, shown standing by a window that did not open. 'Jadyn James is your basic mid-level Secret Service agent. Spent the last four years on counterfeit currency investigations.'

'So . . . Other than this tenuous connection to a pal on the family's security team, there's no previous contact with the VP's family?'

The woman huffed. 'Ask him.'

Carlton went on, 'James is a by-the-book agent. Solid record. Up for promotion to senior status.'

'Past tense,' the woman added. 'No more. He's currently on paid leave.'

Val looked from one to the other. 'And?'

'There's no connection to Russia. Never even been to Europe before now.' Carlton hesitated then said, 'His son . . .'

'Yes? What about the boy?'

'Felix. Eleven years old. Mildly autistic. He copes, but barely.'

'They took an autistic kid to Russia?'

'They did.'

'This makes no sense whatsoever. You know that, don't you?'

Carlton walked back to where he could stab a finger at the man on the console. 'We have got eleven federal employees—'

'Eleven that we know of,' the woman corrected.

'Plus a congresswoman,' the male geek said. 'Bowers. Illinois. Her family. Two adult children, three grandkids. We're almost positive she's gone. Roundabout via Amsterdam and Vienna. But the lady's not talking, and the Russkies don't offer us flight records.'

'Eleven families,' Carlton said. 'And these others. And we've talked with all of them. And we have *no idea* what is going on.'

'We wouldn't know at all if the VP's troublemaker hadn't taken off.' The woman was watching Val now. Her gaze and voice said it all. She shared Carlton's tension and smoldering concern.

Val nodded understanding. If there was anything an intelligence agent hated more than an unanswered question, it was feeling that things were moving out of their control. 'OK. I guess I'm ready.'

When the door clicked shut behind her, Val remained standing in the hotel room's stubby hallway. The closet and bathroom opened to her right. Directly ahead, the agent turned from studying the traffic beyond his window. He nodded in her direction and waited. Patient. Silent. Apparently willing to give her all time in the world.

Val never tired of these first moments. Some nights between writing gigs, when the hours were longest and the dark most intense, she wondered if this was part of why she had such terrible luck with men. She had heard the love songs. Watched the films. Heard how excitement and joy bloomed in that first moment, when love became real, when the heart's flame ignited. When eternity felt within reach.

Hah.

Nothing in her entire existence compared to this high. Standing on the precipice. Surrounded by sheer unknown *potential*. The air thick with promise and danger both. Walking forward meant approaching the death-defying drop, every time as intense as the first. Even more so, really, because now she knew the risks involved.

Experience had shown in vivid detail that the next breath could be her last. The unseen threat, the mystery. All there and ready for her, the long descent into crystal waters, the rocks like daggers poised beneath the surface . . . She loved this more than anything. More than life.

'Agent James, I'm Val Garnier.'

'The journalist.' He nodded. 'Call me Jadyn.'

'You've heard of me?'

'My wife read your book. The one about family life in Afghanistan after the Taliban retook control. It moved her to tears.' He shifted to the table, but stood by the chair facing into the camera, waiting politely. 'How long were you there?'

'The first time, four and a half months. The second, only three weeks. I was kicked out.'

'Hopefully you won't have that trouble this time around.' He gestured toward the chair opposite his. 'I assume that's why we're here. Because you're going.'

'They want me to leave tomorrow.'

'Good. It's the only way you'll understand.'

'I'm sorry. Understand what?'

He merely smiled. 'Why don't we sit down?'

As Val approached the table, the woman's voice sounded in her ear. 'Tell James to replace the heart and oxygen monitor.'

But he was already lifting the finger-clip from its place by the camera stand. He fit it onto his left forefinger, slipped its wire out of the way, and pulled back his chair. Waiting.

Val seated herself and studied the guy. Jadyn James was a typical federal agent. Very fit, very trim, utterly self-contained. African American, late thirties, charcoal suit, a hint of silver in his close-cropped hair. Rather handsome in a thoroughly buttoned-down fashion.

There was no reason why her heart should be hammering so. The agent gave her no reason to be afraid. And she wasn't, not really. It was more the adrenaline surge before battle, the sense that the danger could leap out at any time and consume her.

But there was no reason for this either. None.

She said, 'You know why I'm here.'

'Of course. You want to know why I went to the Kuril Islands.'

'You have to admit, it's very odd.'

'Sure. I get that.' He crossed his legs, straightened the crease of his trousers. 'It's a lot simpler than everyone wants to believe.'

'Will you tell me?'

'Of course.' He turned from her. Looked straight into the camera. 'As often as I need. But nothing's changed from the last time I explained.'

'So tell.'

'Ellen Kavonski is on the vice president's security detail. She and Lauren, the VP's daughter, have become friends. Lauren swore Ellen to secrecy, then confided that she planned to make the trip. She wanted Ellen to come with her. Ellen said she couldn't for a dozen reasons, first and foremost because her husband is undergoing chemo. But Ellen agreed to try and find someone who would respect Lauren's desire for secrecy and keep watch.'

Val made sure her phone's recording app was active, and set it on the table between them. Wondering if he would see it as a challenge. 'That doesn't explain taking your family along.'

'I couldn't agree more. Actually, I was astonished when Ellen approached me. We're not that close. I asked how many other agents she had spoken with. She said I was the first, and that Lauren had suggested me.'

The female techy spoke in Val's ear. 'OK, that's new.'

Val asked, 'Did you know the vice president's daughter?'

'We'd met on a couple of occasions. I served on the advance detail when it was all hands on deck. But no, she was definitely not a friend or anything.'

'Then why?'

He nodded. 'It's a good question, sure enough.'

She waited. Breathing through pursed lips. Trying to fit the confusion into a proper set of questions. Failing. When he remained silent, watchful, she pressed, 'Your family.'

'Right. My son, Felix.'

'He's autistic, correct?'

A flicker of something in his gaze. There and gone. 'Actually, he's one of those who are borderline on the scale. We're biased, of course. But my wife and I like to think he's more Asperger's.'

Val leaned forward. Trying to identify what it was she saw there, almost showing through the professional agent's mask. The only word that came to mind was . . .

Humor.

He was laughing at her.

She straightened. 'What about your son?'

'One of the common traits of Asperger's is the intense focus they put on some things.'

'He wanted to go to the Kurils?'

'Oh no. That doesn't go nearly far enough. For him it wasn't a desire. *He had to go.* When he realized we weren't going, he . . .'

'What?'

'He went ballistic. Totally freaked out. It's the nightmare scenario every parent of an autistic child dreads. He screamed at us for days. Nothing silenced him. We were afraid he was going to wreck his vocal cords.' For once, the agent lost his cool mask. Showed the strains and shadows of a very hard time. 'We finally sedated him. The silence lasted as long as he was in a stupor. Soon as he recovered from the drugs, it started all over again.'

'How long before the agent . . .'

'Nine days. Nine endless, horrible days.'

'I can't imagine what that must have been like for you and your family.'

'No.' His features drumlike with remembered tension. 'You can't.'

'So then the agent spoke with you, and you agreed, and then your son . . .'

'He calmed down instantly. That's another characteristic. Soon as he accepted we were going, he went quiet. Night and day. The tantrums never happened.'

Val watched his features ease, his chest relax, an easy breath. But not her. If anything, the tension heightened. 'How did he know? I mean . . .'

'I know what you mean. The answer is no one knows. Felix's not telling, that's for sure.'

'How was he on the trip?'

'Felix was . . . incredible.' Another smile, this one gentle. The tension utterly gone now. For him. 'He listened. He responded. He obeyed.'

'That's not his common response?'

'Ha.' A pause, then again, 'Ha.'

'And since you've returned?'

'Felix has been fantastic. We keep waiting for the changes to, you know, evaporate. For things to go back to how they were before. But so far, the alterations seem to be at least semi-permanent. His teachers are astonished. They're talking about possibly transitioning him out of special school, into regular classes.' He shook his head. 'My wife and I are afraid to hope.'

'So how was it over there?'

'Oh, it was great. The only island we visited, Kunashir, is unlike any place on Earth. It was formed by four volcanoes that were originally separate islands. Now they're joined together by low-lying areas with lakes and hot springs. These regions form nesting sites for hundreds of thousands of birds.' Another smile, this one easy. The eyes distant now, remembering. 'Felix couldn't get enough of the birds. They loved him. I know that sounds crazy. But they would literally fly up and land on his shoulders, his head, every-where. I've never known my son to be so happy, so totally relaxed. It was . . .'

'What?'

'It was heaven.' He refocused. 'You're going, aren't you?'

'I told you. They want me to leave tomorrow.'

'Good.' He nodded with his entire upper body. Rocking in place. 'Don't wait. The season lasts only a few weeks. Two months tops.

Then it's over. Winter sets in. You don't want to be there when the snows strike. Plus the ferries only operate during good weather.'

She tried to find another question, came up with, 'Why did the VP's daughter want to go?'

He shook his head, still captured by the smile and his son's image. 'She never said. Only that it was something she needed.'

'She *needed* to do this.'

'Right. Whatever her reason, it formed a connection between her and Felix. Shocked the heck out of everybody, I mean, Lauren Dale defines self-absorbed.' He cocked his head, studying the window. 'At least, she did. I hear she's gone through her own set of changes.'

She watched him squint into the sunlight. 'Tell me what you're thinking.'

'Probably nothing.' He refocused on her. 'But that element of self-absorption is a common trait along the autism scale.'

'How did she respond to being there?'

He actually laughed out loud. 'You should have seen her. The two of them, Lauren and Felix, getting smothered by birds. The beasties wouldn't approach the rest of us. But those two, they danced in the nesting areas, and the birds, man, it was almost like they danced with them.'

Val cut off her phone. Defeated. 'Thanks. Is it OK if I contact you again?'

'Oh, sure. When you get back, come over, I'll introduce you to Felix, we'll have dinner.' He rose with her. Studied her a long moment, then offered his hand and said, 'Go. It's the only way you'll ever understand.'

'Understand what?'

He merely smiled and repeated, 'Go.'

SIX

Agnes watched the live feed of Val Garnier's interview alone except for Grey Mathers. She resisted the same urge that had kept her up nights. Put together a full investigative force. Bring in Research and Analysis. Take it to the Homeland director. Give voice to the growing litany of concerns.

But the lack of hard evidence held her back.

In an intelligence world dominated by shadow organizations and terrorist plots, this situation was different. The individuals involved did not show any threat. They did not even appear to associate with one another once they returned home.

When Val rose from the table and the techies next door cut the feed, Agnes asked Grey, 'Any word from your pals in Secret Service?'

'Same as yesterday.' Grey was a solid, careful, painstaking operative. He also possessed a solid background in research and surveillance. The fact that he shared her worries was a distinct comfort. 'Jadyn spends time with his wife and son. He works out. They attended a barbecue my pals put on. Friendly, calm, easy with the time off. Jadyn did ask if they could help him get back on active duty. Nothing more.'

She stared at the blank screen. Saw her worried, angry face glare back. 'What's the latest on the travelers associated with Capitol Hill?'

'Nothing useful. I need more people on this—'

'No. Absolutely not. We can't risk this getting out. Not one *word*. Are we clear?'

'Yes, Director.'

But she wasn't done. 'We are conducting a clandestine survey of people who could very easily have our jobs. We have no evidence of any wrongdoing. There was no reason why they shouldn't have gone on a vacation.'

'To Russia,' Grey said. 'Given our current political situation, I'd say—'

'They returned; they are open about their experience. And what—' She swung her chair around. Faced the agent who shared her angry fear. 'What do we have that might excuse our opening a full-scale covert investigation?'

Grey's jaw muscles bunched and released. Then, 'To answer your question. The congresswoman we've discussed. Her husband and three children. Beyond that, I'm pretty sure we're looking at two other congressmen, a senator, and seventeen senior aides. That's my best guess.'

Agnes felt the fear congeal, turning her gut to ice. 'Twenty-one? Are you serious?'

'And their families. None definite. But yes. I'm fairly certain they've all taken part in whatever this is.'

'You have direct evidence of these people traveling to the Kurils?'

'Of course not. I would have alerted you if I knew for certain. A couple of these families have gone to Taiwan. Most went via Hong Kong. From there they all traveled to northern Japan.' He tapped his tablet, handed it over. 'Summary of private jet manifests. Compliments of my buddies in the NSA. This is as far as I can take it without authorization.'

The list was clear enough. Dates of travel, numbers in each family. Following that, confirmation of private jets flying to Hokkaido within the families' travel dates. And back a few days later. Agnes asked, 'No names?'

'Private jet hires in the Far East don't require passenger names. They leave that to customs.'

'A private jet from Hong Kong to Japan's northern port . . .'

'Between seventy-five and a hundred thousand dollars. Each way.'

'How many Washington staffers can afford that sort of outlay?'

'None, is my guess. Not to mention the congressmen and senator.' Grey ran a large hand through his crewcut. 'What a mess.'

When Agnes handed back the tablet, she realized her hands were shaking. 'Stay on this. Quiet as you can.'

He remained seated. Watching her. 'You're as worried about this as I am.'

Agnes was tempted to tell the agent he had it totally wrong. She wasn't worried. She was borderline terrified.

Of what exactly, she could not say.

When she remained silent, Grey said, 'We need to take this up the ladder.'

'Evidence,' she replied. 'Bring me what I need. Until then, don't breathe a word of this. To anyone.'

SEVEN

Val made a stir-fry of bean sprouts and fresh tofu and broccoli. She boiled a ready-bag of brown rice. She ate an early dinner at her kitchen counter, making notes and moving forward. She was back on the hunt. Routines and disciplines became easier. It was not a conscious decision, something she struggled over, nothing like that. Her life had purpose now. Being clear-headed and relatively healthy was vital to seeing the project through.

She went online, checked out the hotels around Tokyo's Narita airport, selected one, and booked herself in. Two nights. She wanted to be over the worst of jetlag before taking the next step. She was in bed before nine and slept well.

The next morning, Carlton sent a text saying he would accompany her to the airport. Which was a big deal in many respects. Annapolis to Dulles meant a two-hour trek around Washington, fighting traffic and bad highways. She canceled the limo she had booked and finished packing. When she came downstairs, there he was. Same black Lincoln SUV with the tinted windows. The driver-agent opened the rear door, then stowed her case and pack. She greeted Carlton with, 'What, no Grey?'

'Grey stays with the lady. This is Harry. He values silence. That's basically the extent of my knowledge about Harry.'

She gave her upstairs window a final look, a habit that had started so far back she didn't even remember when or why. As if it was important to say farewell to that side of life. Leave it all behind. Focus on getting the story and staying alive.

Carlton waited until they had merged onto the interstate heading west to say, 'You got us good intel back there.'

'Really? I had the impression he was just jumping through hoops.'

'Yes and no. Jadyn didn't say anything that conflicted with what we'd already heard. But this was a fuller response. More personal. Especially that stuff about his son.'

'I should have pressed him again on how Felix found out about it. But Jadyn was on a roll, and I didn't want to interrupt the flow.'

'We assume it was via the internet. Apparently the kid spent hours online.' Carlton glanced over. 'Past tense.'

'It's changed?'

He nodded. 'Felix is doing much better. That's all we have, both from teachers and the docs. They refuse to suggest it's a permanent shift.'

'You interviewed him, I assume.'

'You know, that was interesting. The mother insisted on being present, but otherwise neither she nor Jadyn made any objection. We had the impression they were both glad to have it over and done.'

'And?'

'Felix seemed normal. We had a psychiatrist do the questioning. Afterwards our guy said if he had not read Felix's file he would not have suspected the child to be Asperger's.'

'What, Felix came back from Russia cured?'

'No one is saying that. Yet.'

She swung around in her seat so her back was to the side door and studied the man seated beside her. Carlton had always been straight with her. Not necessarily honest; that would have been asking too much. Plus, for a man like Carlton, honesty was a flexible issue. Honesty was what you gave the public, but only when it matched with what the public wanted to hear. When honesty and political expediency were in conflict, honesty lost out every time.

Carlton endured her assessment for a few minutes, then said, 'Go ahead and ask.'

'There are gaps. Big ones.'

He nodded. 'There are.'

'I'm not talking about what's waiting out there on that island.'

'Kunashir.'

'Right. I'm referring to why I'm here at all. Talking with you. A man who bills out at ten thousand dollars an hour—'

'Please. Don't exaggerate.'

'And who brings along the CIA's deputy director for company.' She crossed her arms. 'I'm waiting.'

He nodded. Once. Twice. Kept his gaze out the front windscreen. Then, 'Three things. No, four.'

'Go on.'

'Like I said, we've sent in four teams.'

'Day before yesterday it was two.'

'I'm not supposed to know about the others. Agnes sent two pairs of Moscow embassy staffers. All came back empty-handed, or so they claim. They talk about the birds. The hot springs. The beauty. The sense of having been cleansed by the experience.'

'You think they're lying.'

'Not exactly. Just not telling the complete truth.'

'That makes no sense.'

He gestured to the road ahead. 'There you go.'

'They're committed professionals. They wouldn't take on an assignment like this and then come back and lie.'

'Now you are precisely where we are.'

'But you're certain they're holding back.'

'Certain? No, Val. We're certain of nothing. But my gut tells me this is happening. And I've had years of trusting my gut.' He waited, and when she remained silent, he went on, 'Point two. Excluding the people Agnes sent, there's a pattern among the families we've identified as having taken this trip.'

'How many are there?'

'We have no idea.' Firm now. Hard and worried and definite. 'We've interviewed thirty-seven.'

'And?'

'One or more of the family are either somewhere along the Asperger's–autistic line, or . . .' He looked at her for the first time. 'You sure you're ready for this?'

'Tell me.'

'They're not entirely intact. Drugs, history of abuse, prison in a few cases . . .'

Harry chimed in from behind the wheel, 'Mental incarceration, three cases of that. All for depression.'

Val said it because she wanted it out there. 'So I fit the stereotype.'

'Yes and no. If all we were looking for was another semi-broken individual, we could have stayed much closer to home. What we needed was something else entirely.' His gaze was clear, level, impersonal. Like seeing sunlight through an ancient glacier. 'We need a highly trained investigator. Someone who has a history of successfully uncovering what others have missed. Who knows how to get in close, and yet remain totally outside the loop.'

She breathed in and out. Hearing it hurt. Just the same . . . 'OK.'

Carlton's only response was another of those slow nods. But Val had the distinct impression that he approved. He went on, 'Point three. We've gone over the video and photo images from these trips that have been posted online. Thoroughly. There appear to be gaps. If the records have been altered, it's a very professional job. More than that. Our experts can't agree that it's actually happened. Even NIS is stumped. But there are small elements that don't add up. Shifts in the sun, days that don't match the length of trips. Like that.'

'You've asked about this.' It was not a question.

'Of course we have. Everyone responds with almost identical words. They shot what was new, then the camera got in the way, and they stopped.'

'Batteries ran down,' Harry offered. 'We've heard that a lot.'

'What about intel from other countries?'

'That's where things get interesting.' Carlton offered a meaning-less smile. 'The answer is we're getting very little. Nothing, really. And this from people I genuinely trust.'

He stopped. Waiting. Clearly wanting her to fill in the blank.

'The techy monitoring James. She said the VP's daughter was the first time they'd heard anything.'

'There you go.'

'You think the other intelligence agencies don't know yet?'

'Don't know, or perhaps they've simply discounted the whole affair. Which would definitely have been our response, had Lauren not made the trip with a Secret Service agent from a different division.'

'You need to tell them.'

'Tell them what? That we're worried?'

'Director Pendalon is debating this very issue.' Harry was engaged now. Watching them in the rearview mirror more than the road. 'Worried if somebody knows more than we do and decides to keep it tight.'

'Doubtful,' Carlton said.

'Still. It could be happening. It's costing Agnes sleep, I can tell you that much.'

Carlton started to say something, then shrugged and turned back to Val. 'Last point. We're hearing rumors from our active sources. This is solid intel, Val. The FSB are growing concerned. About what, we're not sure. We suspect they don't know either.'

The Russian Federation's Federal Security Service, or FSB, had replaced the old intelligence agency known as the KGB. 'Not good.'

'You need to be on the watch for them. If we hear anything definite, we'll let you know.' He lifted his briefcase from the footwell, set it on the seat between them, clicked the locks, and handed her what appeared to be a new phone. 'This is a next-gen satellite phone. It looks and acts exactly like your basic Android model. But this one connects instantly with whatever satellite is within reach. And everything you send, photos, texts, calls, all of it is automatically encrypted.'

She accepted the device. It weighed considerably more than a regular phone, and was such a glossy black it was impossible to tell where the frame ended and the screen began. 'Spies have the coolest toys.'

'Everything you send will be saved and made available upon your return.'

'Promise?'

'You have my word.' He watched Val stow the device in her purse. 'Do you want a gun?'

'Traveling through Japan and Russia? Are you kidding?'

'Probably best.' He studied her a long moment. 'I hate sending you off alone and unprotected.'

The words seemed to vibrate in the air between them. 'I'll be OK,' she replied. Wishing she could manage to keep her voice steady.

EIGHT

Fifteen minutes after Val's too-brief interview with Bernard, their tour guide, they boarded the ferry and set off.

There was not even a hint of wind, which was both good and bad. Good, because the water was calm, the surface blanketed by a pewter sheen. Bad, because the boat taking them to Kunashir Island smelled. The stench was everywhere, and very strong. Every now and then, smoke from the stubby smokestack sank in noxious black clouds. Even so, most of the passengers remained outside, because the fumes from the toilets were indescribable.

Val followed the example of other travelers and wrapped a scarf around her nose and mouth. It helped some. Not a lot. She was seated on the forward bench, just behind the bow anchor. Arbila was beside her, which meant they were joined by a motley crew of other travelers. Val did not mind the company. They had the friendly energy of mutts in heat, minus the lolling tongues and wagging tails.

Except when the Russians closed in.

The four in civilian dress all wore black turtlenecks, black anoraks, black trousers, heavy lace-ups, dark shades. A six-pack of uniformed soldiers followed behind, submachine guns slung over their left shoulders. Half an hour after leaving the port, they began drifting around, demanding papers, asking questions that did not need volume to sound threatening. One by one the travelers around Val reached into their packs and pockets, then dumped their stash over the side. Even so, when the crew started toward the bow, Val's neighbors looked like frightened rabbits.

Finally it was their turn. 'Passports.'

Val and Arbila both had theirs at the ready.

'What is the purpose of your visit to Kunashir?'

Val watched as other passengers offered up passports. Canada, Switzerland, USA, Argentina, Thailand, Morocco. The officials gathered them all, began leafing through pages. She replied, 'I've heard about the nature reserve here for years.'

'There is no nature in your homeland? America is all

paved?' The man was short and solid as a black fireplug. 'A parking lot like the song says?'

'The hot springs are unique,' Val replied. Beside her, Arbila had done the frightened little girl thing, ducking her head and scrunching in small as possible, eyes downcast. Not speaking. Not even breathing. Val went on, 'I've always wanted to see the Kunashir owl.'

'The owl, yes, the owl. Tell me what you know.'

'Blakiston's fish owl is the largest living species, one of the biggest predator birds on Earth. Some think it's a holdover from a prehistoric—'

'Yes, all right. Enough on the owl.' He tapped the pack of passports on his opposing fist. 'All these people, they travel with you to see a bird?'

'I can only speak for the lady here beside me.'

His gaze seemed to remain on Val, but it was hard to be certain with the dark shades. 'All of you are so interested in Russian nature, you travel from around the world?' He gestured to the others. 'Open your cases. All of them.'

The three other agents and the six military made a swift and thorough check. But the short man simply stood there, watching them, studying the horizon, silent. When the last of his men straightened, he demanded, 'How long do you stay?'

'Just three days. Like my visa says.'

'What about the military compound? This interests you also?'

'We arrive in Yuzhno-Kurilsk. We head north. Away from the town and the compound and the soldiers.'

'I am thinking we travel with you. See these birds for ourselves. What do you say to that?'

Val kept her voice steady. 'It's your island.'

'On this you are correct.' He handed her all the passports, and made a threat of his final words. 'Enjoy your stay on our island.'

NINE

A subdued crowd waited to disembark. Being confronted by the FSB had condensed the visitors into tight and worried clusters. The hour was late, close on five in the afternoon. This far north, in July the sun never fully set, so hiking in the dark would not be an issue. But Val was tired, and she was both fit and young. Some of the others, especially the elders who had arrived with the tour group, were flagging.

A military jeep and three trucks with camouflage canvas tops were parked about fifty yards away. Another dozen soldiers stood in two orderly rows. An officer stepped forward and saluted the four Russian civilians in black. They spoke for a long moment while the soldiers who had accompanied them walked down the gangplank and joined the others. Cigarettes were lit. Val saw a couple of smiles, not many. A lot of hard gazes were cast at the tourists gathered along the ship's rail.

Val had once written a long article on life in the Inuit settlements. She had spent seven hard months living with them. The harbor town of Yuzhno-Kurilsk reminded Val of those hardscrabble Alaskan communities. The houses she could see were all built of some corrugated material, most with metal tie-downs anchoring the roofs, a clear indication of the punch carried by winter storms. All the northern walls were insulated with wood chopped and piled and drying for the season which was never far away. The fishing boats in the harbor shared the same weary, weather-beaten look as the houses.

She liked the smells. Wood fires, some coal, diesel, and fish and drying nets and seaweed. Ocean salt spiced the fragrances. She breathed deep, excited and glad to be here. The soldiers did not scare her, mostly because Bernard, their unofficial guide, stood by the gangplank, calmly watching the scene. She was tempted to walk over, press for answers. But the man had already shown her the ability to deflect. Cool and patient and intelligent and totally in control. Such people made for terrible interviews.

The fireplug agent waved to the skipper watching from the ferry's wheelhouse. The boat's whistle blasted a single long note. Bernard called, 'All right, everyone. Let's get started.'

Three tractors were parked at the harbor's furthest corner, as far from the military vehicles as they could get and still stay on the pavement. Two men and a woman sat on the curved metal seats. All three wore denim trousers and jackets. The woman's only flash of color was a scarf wrapped over her hair. All of the tractors were hooked to wooden flatbed trailers, probably used for hauling nets and their catch. Then one of the men spotted Bernard coming down the gangplank. He whistled, waved, and started his tractor.

Instantly the fireplug agent stomped over and shouted. The tractor driver called back, grinning. When the agent barked again, the driver rubbed his thumb and forefinger together, indicating payment. The agent did not like it, especially when Bernard walked up and shook hands with all three drivers.

Bernard then waved the tourists forward. 'Pile into the back. Make yourselves comfortable. We have a ways to go.'

They made an odd little convoy leaving the township. Three tractors trundled along at barely above a walking pace. The jeep and military trucks followed not far behind. Bernard rode standing on the first tractor's sideboard, chatting and laughing with the driver. Very easy with the journey and the day. His attitude telling anyone who looked his way that everything was cool.

An hour north of Yuzhno-Kurilsk, the road simply ended. The tractors continued on, rocking and rolling over a rutted trail. The way was pitted and the going very slow. Val lay down and watched the sky. Clouds were thin as veils, a softening of the blue more than any real color. The tractors rumbled and the trailer rocked and jostled her against Arbila on one side and one of the male trekkers on her left. She must have fallen asleep, because the next thing she knew the sun had lowered to within a few degrees of the western horizon. The air was cold now, not much above freezing. Val rose to a seated position and pulled another layer from her pack. Only then did she realize they were crossing a broad stream or shallow river, maybe fifty feet wide, the water thigh deep at most. The tractors took it at a slow steady pace. Once they reached the other side, their driver rose in his seat and shouted back at the military vehicles still parked on the stream's other side. He pointed to a path they should take, then continued guiding them with hand gestures until the military vehicles had

safely crossed. The first truck's driver responded by grinning out
his window, shouting what was probably thanks, and offering a
gloved thumbs-up.

All good pals.

Val stretched out again, but she did not sleep. The air was biting
now. In late July. She wondered if they were supposed to sleep
outside. She wondered if the nesting birds were for real. All she
had seen so far were gulls drifting overhead, heads swiveling, alert
for any scraps the travelers might offer.

Then she smelled food.

Cooking food.

Hot food.

She had not realized until then how famished she had become.
Probably being 'fronted by Russian agents on the border of nowhere
would do that to an appetite.

She was not the only one who sat up and craned forward. What
she saw . . .

The campsite was beyond orderly. A double circle of conical
tents. Two central cooking fires. A trio of men and two women busy
with huge cooking ladles, stirring four massive kettles, working the
grills, turning kebabs.

All the comforts of home.

One of the women came over, in her forties with a well-worn
face. She hugged Bernard, then together they started toward the
military vehicles. Val slipped down and walked on unsteady legs
over to where she could hear Bernard addressing the agents in what
sounded like fluent Russian. He and the woman gestured to the
fires, the food, the tents. Then they started back, and the woman
said to the tourists, 'Welcome to Kunashir Island. You can wash in
the stream there to your left. Latrines are along the path to
your right. Women's tents are marked with a strip of green tape
above the portals. Find a spot, drop your bags, then come eat.'

Val heard one of her fellow trekkers call, 'We're not part of
the tour group.'

'Did I ask how you got here?' She waved an easy hand. 'Make
yourselves at home.'

They dined on a thick vegetarian stew and kebabs of smoked fish
with fresh wild greens. Tea with honey for dessert. Val studied the
other newly arrived travelers as she ate. Most were clearly exhausted,
the older people struggling to stay awake, many of the younger ones

coming down from their highs, missing the stash they had deposited in the sea.

And yet . . .

There was a tension, an almost palpable force they all seemed to share. All, that is, save Val. She could see it in their faces, the electric spark to weary gazes, the way they kept shooting glances down trails leading from the camp.

Waiting.

The tractor drivers ate with them, then they offloaded crates of more supplies and headed back. The soldiers came over in clumps of three or four, shyly grateful for the food. The agents came, glared, refused to eat with the others. After everyone finished, volunteers made quick work of cleaning up. Then Bernard and the woman whose name was Iris slipped into tents and emerged wearing sneakers and swimwear. In an evening where the temp was low enough to bite.

Bernard said, 'We're heading for the hot springs. Anyone who wants is welcome to join us.'

Val could see how many wanted to ask, protest, question. Something. But all it took was for the woman playing host to point in the direction of the Russian soldiers. The questions went unasked.

In the end, everyone went. Even the oldest and most weary. All save the military. A pair of the agents trailed along, still in their somber black. They stood at the periphery and watched. For the others, including Val, their presence soon stopped mattering.

The baths were arrayed in a series of circular stone ledges, climbing a rocky cliff face like giant stairs. Streams flowed to either side, cold and clear, forming a trio of waterfalls that sang a musical welcome. The newcomers stood at the boundary as Bernard and Iris pointed out the lukewarm baths, the ones closer to scalding, and three off to one side bearing crude hand-painted skull-and-cross-bones. Steam rose from those in sulfurous waves.

Val chose one where she and Arbila could join a pair of older women, effectively shutting out any of the mongrel trekkers. The feeling was . . .

Exquisite.

She floated for what seemed like hours. A timeless, weightless moment, floating in some otherworldly void while the steam rose and warmed the air. Val shared a long look with Arbila, and the young woman revealed an almost childlike smile. Happy.

They emerged and showered in the frigid waterfall, then walked back to camp. Utterly exhausted. Thoroughly refreshed. Completely able to disregard the black-clad agents and the soldiers they had set on patrol around the camp's periphery.

There weren't enough towels, so she and Arbila shared one, laughing as they dried off, then climbing into the yurt-shaped tent. Dressing in sweats and heavy woolen socks. Choosing bedrolls from those stacked nearby. Unfurling and slipping inside.

Bang and gone.

The next thing Val knew, Iris was kneeling by the door, wiggling both her foot and Arbila's. When they were both more or less awake, Iris said, 'It's time.'

TEN

They made a long column, everyone from both groups moving quiet as possible from the camp. They followed a narrow trail past two uniformed sentries and one agent; all three of them were asleep. The soldiers lay in the scrub, the agent rested against a tree. Totally zonked. Not moving a muscle, not even when one of the older men entered a coughing fit. Val tensed in fear, but Iris continued leading them forward, with Bernard taking up the rear.

They entered a wide plain that circled a crescent-shaped lake. Then into a line of stunted firs that looked identical to the ones Val had last seen in Alaska. Out the other side, further through the scrub and summertime brush, when . . .

A glow appeared up ahead.

Golden, like a giant lantern. Not a fire, though, because it didn't flicker. The illumination turned everything Val saw into something else, as if she peered at a different world. It was impossible to consciously explain what she thought or felt. Only that the light made things *different*.

Before leaving the tent, she had waited until Arbila was outside, then slipped the satellite phone from her pack. Now she powered it up and turned on the camera. She checked before and behind, but all the faces she saw were focused on the glow up ahead. She held it down by her leg, the camera aimed forward, and kept moving forward.

They entered a clearing. And . . .

What she saw . . .

She had once trekked into the Afghan highland. The family she'd been staying with had invited her to a clan gathering. Far removed from the Taliban and the danger they had brought back to the cities and low-lying districts. The trek had been the hardest thing she had ever done, and she had been wearing boots and good Western hiking gear. Following a man twice her age, more, in traditional garb and worn leather sandals. They had rounded just another corner, following an endless winding mountain path, and . . .

The world had dropped away.

An eagle hovered directly in front of her, the wings burnished
by a brilliant noonday sun. The raptor had turned and stared at
her, its eyes golden and fierce. Val had stood there for an endless
time, mesmerized by the beauty and the raw glory of nature at
its harshest. And its finest. When she finally blinked and refocused
on the world, she realized the entire clan was watching her.
Smiling. The old man had said, 'Welcome to Afghanistan.' And
led them on.

That memory popped into her mind as she stood there. Another
experience she could not describe, nor really even take in. She would
need a day back in the real world. A month. A year. Longer.

The clearing was a circle, big as the camp. Bigger. The ground
was covered with the same low scrub, only here it was as manicured
as a formal garden.

The periphery was lined with crystal trees.

They stood about five feet apart and rose just over her head in
height, call it six feet. They formed a mimic of the island's stunted
firs. A boundary fence of glass.

Val approached the nearest and ran a tentative hand along the
trunk. It was not carved. The surface held the polished luster of
hand-blown glass. Multiple branches sprouted just overhead, holding
the slender grace of a young sapling.

But what was most astonishing was how no one else paid the
crystal sculptures any mind whatsoever. Instead . . .

In the clearing's heart stood a tree. She thought it might be a
rowan, but she was not a specialist. Certainly not a type she would
have expected to find on an island this close to the Arctic Circle.
The trunk was so thick she and a couple of the others could not
have encircled it with their outstretched arms. The limbs formed a
graceful canopy, the leaves . . .

Were on fire.

The light was not so much blinding as magnetic. Brilliant and
yet welcoming.

Then she felt it.

The draw was unlike anything she had ever experienced.
Enormously compelling. And yet . . .

There was no sense of being pulled against her will. Strong as
it was, she felt totally able to say no.

Which was what she did.

Val took a step back. Another. Until the ring of crystal trees stood between her and all the others. None of them even looked her way. Their attention was totally focused on the tree with its glowing, shimmering leaves.

Then one of them – Val realized it was Iris – reached up and plucked a leaf.

She brought the glowing leaf up to her forehead. As she did . . .

The leaf became transformed. The glow strengthened. It formed . . .

A rope. Or a thread. Or streamer. Of golden light. One that wrapped itself around her head.

And disappeared.

The light, however, remained. All of Iris glowed now. A brilliant human lantern. Or flameless torch. Or beacon. Something. All the words fit, and none of them did. Not entirely.

Val watched as Iris stepped back, making room for the throng who surged forward as . . .

The tree's branches lowered down. Bringing the leaves into the reach of the smallest. The most aged. The ones bowed by the day and the trip and life. The youngest. They all took leaves.

The urge to walk forward, join them, claim a leaf or whatever it was, grew in Val until she struggled not to weep. Still, she held back. Even now, when conscious thought was reduced to fragmented yearnings, she remained the investigative journalist. The professional observer. Though her stance beyond the trees left her feverish with longing.

She watched as some wrapped the coils of light around their arms. Or just stood there looking at this bit of gleaming whatever in their hands. The leaves became threads, and the threads encircled whatever was closest. Hands, arms, necks, foreheads. Until all the people were glowing like Iris.

All save Val.

She video-recorded a continuous run, holding it just below the level of her chin. Swinging back and forth. She watched Bernard take a leaf, wait while the thread took its glowing form, then simply lift it and breathe it in.

When he was fully illuminated, he started back toward her.

Val readied herself for a fight, argument, condemnation. Whatever. Instead, he asked, 'Would you like me to hold that while you go?'

She wanted to. More than anything. And yet . . .

'That's not why I made this trip.'

He shifted over and stood there beside her. Bathing Val's right side in a glow that warmed her from the heart outwards. Making the hunger stronger still. 'Why are you here, Val?'

'You know the answer to that.'

'Do I?' He smiled at her. 'Do you?'

'I'm writing this up.' Almost defying him to object.

'And this writing, does it deny you the opportunity to experience? Are you forbidden, Val?'

'A journalist is required to remain objective.'

'But a journalist must also understand, no?' He gestured to the tree. 'This is ending, Val.'

'Ending? How?'

'As far as you're concerned, this experience, this opportunity, could very well be now or never.'

Iris walked over and positioned herself on Bernard's other side. She probably intended for her words not to carry. But Val was a pro at overhearing conversations. Iris asked, 'She didn't take it?'

'Not yet.'

'Not *yet*? There is no tomorrow, Bernard.'

'We don't know that.'

'What I do know is we need her.'

'There may still be a chance.'

Iris stepped forward far enough to glare at Val. 'Are you certain you're doing the right thing?'

Val did not find herself able to respond.

Iris glowered another long moment, her gaze molten in the tree's light. Finally she broke off and started towards the group.

Iris clapped her hands several times, and called, 'Pay attention, everyone.'

When the others continued to meander about, or stroke the tree trunk, Iris shouted, '*Wake up!*'

The words as well as the tone somehow pushed Val into journalist mode. Did this mean they had all been in a trance? Caused by what? The leaf?

Bernard's warning pierced her questions, something few things did. Now or never *for what*?

She saw how the people closest to her gradually came to full alert, and she knew an instant of genuine panic. The draw from the tree was strong as ever, an invitation as clear and precise as anything she had ever experienced.

Then the moment was over. Iris and Bernard moved through the crowd, ensuring everyone was clear-eyed, focused, and *there*.

Then, as the crowd reluctantly retreated . . .

All the surrounding crystal trees shattered.

The shards fell like a circular rain. There was no wind, so the remnants lay in an almost perfect circle, shimmering in the tree's reflected light.

The group gave off a soft moan that Val felt in her bones. Val did not understand, nor was she truly part of whatever was happening. Just the same, she was captivated by a sense of . . .

Departure.

Then the tree itself became something else entirely. Before, the illumination was softly welcoming. Now . . .

A great rushing flame rose from the earth, consuming it from the trunk outwards. And yet . . .

There was no danger here. Nor heat.

Val found herself recalling what Bernard had said when they had stood together outside the Russian port building.

Inevitable.

That was how it felt. There was no logic to her notion. Just the same, she had the strong impression that everyone around her felt as she did. No sorrow, not even surprise. The tree simply ceased to belong.

The trunk and then the branches flamed with a light so brilliant it hurt to watch. But she remained as she was, squinting with the hand not holding her phone. Watching as . . .

The silent flame consumed the tree. And the remnants of the surrounding crystal trees. All of it. Gone. Except . . .

A soft cloud of glowing leaves drifted to the earth.

Iris was already moving. 'Gather up all you can.' She and Bernard pulled black plastic garbage bags from their packs and began handing them out. 'Hurry now.'

Everyone rushed forward, sweeping up great armfuls of the glowing leaves. Gradually the light diminished until there was nothing left. Just leaves colored like autumn russet. Filling the arms of all the people present. Except for her.

Iris said, 'Pay attention, everyone. We're going back to the camp. Then we depart.'

One of the older men said, 'I'm very tired.'

'I know you are. And there's nothing to be done about it. If you remain, the agents will be asking questions. Hard questions. That is why they came. To observe, and then tomorrow to begin interrogations. If you stay, you may not survive their questions.' She gave that a beat, then said, 'Let's move. We have to hurry if we're going to stay safe.'

Tired as they all were, they made good time. When she was back inside their tent, Val emptied her pack of everything save one change of clean clothes, her money and ID, and her laptop. She then stuffed inside most of the leaves she had brought back. Arbila and the other woman who shared their tent watched Val, but neither made any objection. Whatever they felt, sharing this journey with one woman who refused to do what had all brought them together, they did not say. Even so, as they emerged from the tents, Val felt as if she carried a shadow. One she had been building all her life. One shred of dark thread at a time. Never noticed until now. Not really. What she recalled when she allowed herself to look back were the mistakes. The wrong moves. The bad men.

This was different.

As she joined the others, Val felt as though she had lost a chance to set all those burdens down. Instead, she had merely followed a lifelong pattern. Another experience, another dark thread. Weaving itself around her mind, her heart, her life.

They followed Iris away from the camp and the still-slumbering soldiers and agents, and clambered into the military trucks.

Bernard started the motor, Val climbed into the back, and they all watched and waited until Iris called softly, 'That's everyone.'

They headed east. Away from the port. Into a vague and silent dawn.

Three hours later they pulled up in front of a beach of rocky shale. Six highly sophisticated craft idled at the water's edge. They were dark, large, professional boats, between twenty and thirty feet long and powered by massive Honda outboards. Three were skippered by men, three by women. Bernard and Iris gently, firmly, hurriedly moved their charges over the uneven rocks, made slippery with seaweed and moisture, down to where the boats' skippers helped them on board.

Soon as everyone had a place, the boats pushed off and headed south by east. Crossing the forbidden Kuril Straits. Out of Russian territory. Towards the looming mountains of Hokkaido. And Japan. And safety.

ELEVEN

The day after Val's return from Japan, Carlton asked the driver to drop him off three blocks from the Eisenhower Building. A limo stopping directly in front of the main entrances inevitably drew crowds. Nowadays most of these onlookers lifted phones and snapped his photo. When they didn't recognize him as someone with clout, they turned away disappointed. Carlton hated the theater surrounding politics in DC. So unless the weather was dreadful, he approached on foot.

Most long-term insiders still referred to the structure as the Old Executive Office Building. Connected to the White House by two sidewalks and an underground tunnel, the OEOB took sixteen years to build, and during its construction became the capitol's most controversial structure. Mark Twain referred to it as 'the ugliest building in America.' The press despised it. The public was split down the middle, with the well-educated and powerful wanting it torn down and replaced with something more suitable. Their vociferous criticism led Alfred Mullett, its architect, to commit suicide. But not even that halted the censure. The historian Henry Adams called it an 'architectural insane asylum'. Harry Truman called it a monstrosity and refused to enter.

Carlton thought it was wonderful.

The French Empire style meant it clashed with every other building in the city. In its early days, the OEOB housed the State Department, the Navy, and the Army. Nowadays it held White House staffers without enough clout to claim an office next door.

Carlton greeted the aide waiting in the marble-tiled lobby, accepted his pass, and followed the young man along the broad ground-floor corridor, down to the building's largest conference room. There were only five people waiting for him. But one of them was the Vice President of the United States, who had insisted on holding this conference away from his main offices in the White House and Congress. Carlton had known VP Terrance Dale for over twenty years, and liked and respected the man. Soon as the aide closed the door and seated himself by the exit, CIA Deputy Director Agnes Pendalon snapped, 'Report.'

Carlton ignored the woman's impatience. He greeted the VP, shook hands with the young aide seated behind Terrance, then made his way around the table's vast expanse, taking time to admire the three chandeliers, the tall sash windows with the White House peeking through the trees. By the time he seated himself with his back to the summertime green, he thought Agnes Pendalon looked parboiled.

He described his meeting with Valentina Garnier. Val had returned from Japan the previous evening, and agreed to meet Carlton only if it happened in her apartment. Her verbal account mirrored the images she had uploaded to the hovering satellite. The main difference was her emotional state. He left that out. For the moment.

When he went quiet, Agnes gave the VP a chance to speak, then demanded, 'How did she appear to you?'

'Exhausted. Utterly shattered.'

Terrance Dale spoke for the first time. 'Hardly a surprise. Annapolis to Japan to Russia and back, all in how long?'

'Six and a half days,' Carlton replied. 'It was more than the trip.'

Agnes could sneer with the best of them. 'You're oh so certain of that, are you?'

'I am. Yes.' He found it easier to focus on the vice president. 'I've known Val for almost ten years. Before today, I would have said that almost nothing about a story carried the force to rock her world.'

'Hardly a surprise, given what she's witnessed.' Terrance Dale asked Agnes, 'Any further response from your team over who or what might be at work here?'

'Sir, my team consists of myself, Agent Grey Mathers, my driver, and two technicians. To give this the attention it deserves, I need to bring in further resources.'

'We've been over this. Your request is denied. For the moment.'

'Sir—'

'How am I supposed to justify a full investigation? Show images of a tree on a Russian island that visitors find appealing? Especially now that the tree has apparently vanished.'

'Mister Vice President, if you would allow us—'

'Your request is denied.' He turned back to Carlton. 'You were saying the experience rocked her world. Unpack that a little.'

Carlton recalled the way she had looked at the end of their time together. She had walked him to the door, then offered a farewell that he found grave and somber and tragic. Val had actually embraced him. There had been such a strong sense of finality, Carlton had experienced severe heartache the entire journey back to DC. 'She reminded me of a strong woman in mourning. Getting on with life. But barely. Every step, every word, cost her.'

Agnes sighed. Shook her head. Opened the file on the table in front of her and started making notes.

Terrance Dale studied the CIA deputy director, his face impassive. 'Any sign of alarm from Moscow?'

'Nothing, sir.' Agnes continued making notes. 'Not a peep.'

'You'd expect a mass disappearance in the company of FSB agents to set off a five-alarm response.'

'Yes, sir. You would.' Agnes set down her pen. Met the VP's gaze. 'But nothing about these incidents meets expectations. Which is why I feel you should authorize a full covert investigation.'

'On what grounds? People travel to Kunashir and come back happy?'

'Sir, we are facing a potentially catastrophic—'

'You have no evidence of that, Agent Pendalon. None whatsoever.'

'Just the same, sir, you were concerned enough about your own daughter's—'

'Concerned. Yes. So I approached Carlton. Asked him to look into it. At his insistence, I alerted you. And here we are.'

'Sir, I can take this no further without—'

'Without turning this into another three-ring circus. Can you imagine what the public's response would be? Because you and I both know this would get out. The White House is leakier than my brother's sailboat. Which sank.'

Agnes dropped her gaze back to the open file and her notes. Sighed a second time.

Dale continued, 'We have nothing, repeat nothing, that justifies taking this any further. Am I concerned? Absolutely. But to have Homeland open an official investigation, we need proof of something that points to a genuine threat. Do you have proof, Agent Pendalon?'

'Not yet, sir. And to find it, I need more resources than—'

'Proof. Bring me something concrete, you'll get everything you want.' The VP turned back to Carlton and asked, 'How did Ms Garnier respond when you informed her the lab results on her leaf? What was the tree again?'

The VP's aide was a sharp-faced young woman seated by the wall behind his chair. 'A rowan. Common to Russian forests in the southwestern steppes. Very rare that far east. And its size was an astonishment. That was the word the experts used.'

Agnes said, 'I hope your people know to keep this quiet.'

'They were shown still photographs of a tree and told where it had been located,' the aide replied. 'Nothing more.'

Vice President Terrance Dale was the former governor of Vermont. His forebears had farmed the same acreage since colonial days. He represented the party's middle of the road. His stance was a liability in the primaries, which meant he would never rise to the top job. But these same centrist voters were crucial to winning any general election. Which was why he held the position he did, despite the fact that the president loathed him. Dale was steady, strong, principled, unbending on moral issues. Carlton had rarely seen him lose his temper. Or laugh, for that matter. 'My wife tells me the rowan holds a spiritual significance in many cultures, one going back centuries.'

'Longer,' his aide offered. 'There are prehistoric images in Germanic caves. Written records from the Vikings over a thousand years old, calling it the sacred tree.'

'Val mentioned that,' Carlton said.

Agnes looked up. 'Why are we only hearing that now?'

'Because she discounted it as an unimportant sidebar. And so do I. She insists there was nothing religious about the events.'

'Not to mention the glass trees around the periphery,' Terrance Dale added. 'That spooked me, I have to admit.'

'Your daughter never said anything about them?'

'She has not said anything about the tree, or the leaves. Nothing. My wife phoned her last night and asked. Again. Lauren simply replied that it wasn't relevant.' Dale shrugged. 'We're talking about a child who has been my family's living nightmare for nine endless years. Who is now studying for a doctorate in oceanography.'

Agnes said, 'We need to bring Val Garnier into Langley for questioning.'

'What a swell idea,' Carlton replied. 'Pick a Pulitzer Prize-winning journalist off the street. Bring her in against her will. Which this absolutely would be. Haul her off to CIA headquarters. Hold her there without recourse to an attorney, or even being placed under arrest.'

Agnes bristled at his open challenge. 'I assume even you have heard of the Terrorist Act.'

'Outstanding,' he snapped. 'She's outwitted you once already. You don't think she would be prepared for this?'

Dale asked, 'What form would that take?'

'I could think of any number of possibilities. All of them horrible, as far as your administration is concerned. She probably has a number she must call every day and offer a specific verbal code, else her staffer in Singapore or wherever puts it out to the press and the websites that she's been abducted by the same people who sent her to Russia. Including you, Mr Vice President. Keep in mind, she recorded all our conversations, and she's already downloaded the video she captured in Russia. All of a sudden the White House and the CIA would become the center of her story.' Carlton glared across the table. 'Not to mention how you'd be trampling on her basic human rights.'

Agnes Pendalon showed him a cold fury. 'I didn't realize you'd gone over to the dark side.'

'I'm where I've always been. A fervent backer of the rule of law. In case you've forgotten, our Constitution guarantees the same rights to every citizen, regardless of their position or their power.'

Agnes dropped her gaze back to the file. 'Whatever.'

'May I remind you, Madam Deputy Director, the lady has done exactly what you personally told her to. She has captured intel we did not have. She has endured something that threatens to tear her apart. She has done this without complaint.' Carlton gave her a chance to respond, then finished, 'I hope you treat your own subordinates better than this.'

'All right, that's enough,' Dale said.

'Valentina Garnier should be rewarded—'

'I said, enough.' When the VP was certain Carlton had been silenced, he said, 'Back to my question. What was her reaction when you told her about our lab claiming the leaf is just that? A leaf?'

'To be frank, sir, I don't think she cared one way or the other.'

Agnes sniffed, but did not lift her gaze. 'Doesn't sound like much of a journalist.'

'That's not it. She made a note. And then she seemed to dismiss the news. As if it did not really change anything.'

Terrance Dale gave that a moment, then said, 'Tell me what she thought happened out there. More importantly, how does this impact America?'

Carlton nodded. 'I asked the very same thing. Val says that's exactly where she is going to focus.'

'Did she say how?'

'She left Hokkaido with the names and addresses of everyone who made the return trip. She intends to interview them all.'

'She'll keep you informed?'

'Val promised as much.'

'We need to show her captured video to the Secret Service agent who accompanied my daughter, what's his name?'

'Jadyn James,' Agnes replied. 'On it.'

'I think we've taken this as far as we can today.' Terrance Dale rose to his feet. 'And Agnes. I happen to agree with our associate. You and the Agency are hereby ordered to keep your hands off Valentina Garnier.'

Carlton took that as his dismissal, rose from his seat, and followed Terrance and the young aide. But as he approached the exit, the VP asked, 'Other than these interviews, what do you think she will do next?'

Carlton didn't think. He knew.

He was also certain that sooner or later he would share that item with the VP. If anyone deserved to know, it was him.

But not Agnes. Not after how the lady just revealed her true colors. Not in a billion years.

Carlton replied, 'I have no idea.'

TWELVE

After Carlton left her apartment that morning, Val returned to her chair on the condo's stubby balcony. She found herself thinking back to her first glimpse of the dark SUV parked on the side street, all those eons ago. So much had happened. It no longer mattered the number of days that had passed. The intensity of her experiences had managed to expand time. There was no way those few days could contain everything she had been through.

The previous night Val had dreamed of the tree. Only this time, the entity or whatever it was had gained the power of speech. It whispered to her, or tried to. A soft message of hope or change or healing. All of the words seemed to fit, and yet none of them were adequate. When she woke up, she discovered her pillow was drenched with tears of longing.

Val sat in the sullen heat and pondered the impossible. Her heart had been shattered by a tree that was no more.

She was tempted to gather her remaining strength, walk into the kitchen, pull down her secret stash, and put together a concoction strong enough to erase the day. The wrong moves of her life stretched out like a dark path she had wandered in determined blindness. The bond to her late mother had never felt stronger. Nor had the temptation to follow the same course. Continue the family tradition. Give in to the welcome embrace of no longer needing to confront another day.

The late morning was heavy with heat and humidity. Clouds bunched like muscled fists, determined to lock the city in perpetual gloom. She pursed her lips, breathed in and out, wishing she had begged Carlton to stay. He would have remained, despite his need to report in. She had seen the deep concern in his gaze, the regret they had shared over sending her on this impossible mission.

Chasing just another story. Hah.

The dream returned to her then, brilliantly intense. And for the first time since leaving the island, Val was filled with a sense of forward motion. Strong enough to draw her from the chair. Give a definition to the day.

Val opened her laptop and began writing her article.

She was far too short of hard evidence to be doing this. Weeks, perhaps even months before where she should be. Just the same, she had no choice. It had to be now.

With every word she typed, the vivid clarity of this new path grew ever stronger.

She was going to do it.

Take the plunge. Find Bernard, travel to wherever he might be located. Have him activate one of those leaves she had carried back. Turn it into the golden thread or whatever it was. Attach it to herself.

That is, assuming she still had the chance.

Every time she recalled Bernard's warning, that it might all be too late, she broke out in a cold sweat.

Which did not erase her terror. The prospect of taking this step left her positively quaking in her slippers.

Just the same, it was happening.

Which meant the initial article had to be written and done and set in a secure place.

In case she couldn't write it after.

The thought of possibly losing her one solitary gift, her journalistic ability, left her terrified. Her gut felt like ice.

But that changed nothing.

THIRTEEN

Val did not merely write the article. She relived the events. Describing her decision not to accept a leaf, ingest the thread or whatever it was, created a remorse strong as acid.

It remained with her as she wrote about their return journey. The tenders that had taken them to Japan were manufactured by a UK company called RIB, used primarily by owners of superyachts. Carbon-fiber hulls with inflatable gunwales. Super-lightweight, very stable, virtually impossible to capsize, extremely expensive. The nine-meter version with the Honda outboard retailed for almost two hundred thousand dollars.

Six of them had been used to ferry the group away from Kunashir Island.

Where had they come from? How had they known to arrive at that specific time and point for the pickup? What happened to the boats after? She had seated herself on the central bench, between the boat's skipper and Bernard. She kept her voice quiet, shifting back and forth between the two men, pressing them with her questions. Or trying to. When she finally went quiet, the skipper had offered a smile nearly identical to Bernard's. 'Those are all very good questions.'

The motor's soft rumble kept their conversation reasonably private. 'So you're not telling me?'

Bernard replied, 'You had your chance to discover the answers for yourself.'

OK, that stung. 'Turn myself into some magical creature? Go flying off to never-never land?'

'Magic is just a word for science we don't yet understand,' Bernard replied.

The skipper lifted one hand from the wheel and pointed north. 'Never-never land is disappearing out behind us.'

'Come on, guys. Give me something I can use.'

Bernard nodded. 'Which was precisely what we tried to do on the island.'

'Answers,' she pressed. 'How did you get involved with this?'

Bernard kept his gaze on the far horizon. 'How many times have you asked that question?'

'A lot. Dozens.'

'And what answer have you had?'

'They've all felt some kind of draw to the place. Nothing more.'

'Because there's nothing else that can be said,' Bernard replied. 'Until you see for yourself.'

'See *what*?' When both men remained silent, she asked, 'Why are some people drawn here and not others?'

The skipper replied, 'Maybe what you should be asking is, what if the invitation is universal?'

Bernard added, 'Why did some people hear the invitation and not others?'

Val studied the two men, their faces shadowy in the dim light. Strong, intelligent, aware, calm. Very different, yet holding to some strange parallel force . . . 'Who made the invitation?'

Bernard looked at her for the first time since boarding the vessel. 'Maybe that's why you're here. To shape that answer in words others will understand.'

The skipper leaned forward so as to look around her. 'You think?'

'She's definitely here for a reason. She's a professional journalist, an expert at shaping the impossible into words.'

The skipper resumed his scanning of the southern horizon. 'Good point.'

'Guys, please. Give the journalist a break here. I can't do my job without answers!'

'Why don't you take a couple of days,' Bernard replied. 'Think over what you've witnessed. And the step you didn't take. When you're ready, if you're ready, we'll talk more.'

'Another good point,' the skipper said.

Those were the last words either man uttered. Val spent the rest of the voyage seated in the stern beside Bernard, in case he offered something useful, which he didn't. Watching the northern port on Hokkaido Island gradually appear in the mist. Feeling encased within the same blanket of shadows she felt now. Invisible yet present, marring her vision and her future and her internal state.

Val's preliminary article was punctuated throughout by questions like those she had asked on the boat to Hokkaido. She made no bones about not having answers. She also was completely open in why she was making this step. Writing the article now. Before she was anywhere near ready. Because soon as she finished . . .

She spent a long time detailing her contact with Arbila, both before and after. The woman's transformation now formed the backdrop to Val's determination to take this next step.

Standing there on the Hokkaido dock, waiting for transport to the island's main airport, Arbila had been frank and oblique at the same time. Very much like Bernard. The lovely young woman could point to no specific change, other than how she felt good. Happy. Content. Words she almost never used to describe herself. Especially not when she was straight. Which she was.

Interestingly, the attitude shown by the young men had changed as well. They were easy around Arbila, but without any of the sexual hunger they had previously shown. And no drugs. As far as Val could tell, no one used. Or even mentioned it in passing. No apparent regret over how they had dumped their stashes over the ferry's side. How they missed it. How much they had lost. Nothing.

But the primary image, the one that floated up every time Val stopped typing, was when she had asked Arbila why she had done it. Walked forward, taken the leaf, watched it form that golden thread, allowed it to wrap itself around her wrist.

Why?

Arbila had shown her a gaze that defined bottomless. And said, 'You mean, why risk my life?'

'Right. Or whatever. Doing the unknown.'

'What exactly was I risking? Isn't that the first question you need to ask? The great life I'd been having up to that point? All the fun, all the messy nights and hungover days, all the memories that hurt? Why did I not want to hold on to all that?'

'You mean, it's gone?'

'No, Val. Nothing's lost. And that's not the point.'

'So tell me.'

'You don't get it. *That's* the point. I didn't risk anything.'

Val felt defeated. 'No. You're right. I don't understand.'

'I didn't risk. I *invited*.'

'Invited *what*?'

Arbila smiled then. The little-girl smile. Quietly happy. Totally open. 'You need to do this, Val. You really do.'

* * *

Val found it impossible to write in temporal sequence. Instead, her article followed certain themes. Going back over and over the same ground, each time focusing on something else. It was how she recalled the events. She went with her gut, which told her she remembered piecemeal because this was the only way to make sense of it all. Breaking it down into fractions. Taking it all the way to where she met the wall formed by questions with no answers. Then going back. Starting over with a different theme, different perspective.

Once she was done describing the before-and-after Arbila, she returned to the leaves. Repeating her observations of the giant rowan, its glow reflected in the crystal trees. Watching the limbs bend down to where each person could select a leaf all their own. Seeing it become a thread, forging a link to the unknown.

Repeating here what Arbila said. *She invited.* A major question.

On the bus to the airport, Val had asked Bernard if she could hold on to some of the leaves. For research, was how she put it. Waiting for him to demand to know what sort of research she envisioned, and by whom. Instead, the guy offered that same maddening smile and said, 'Many as you like.' He then lifted his voice and said, 'Same goes for the rest of you. Just give us all those you don't want.'

And now. Carlton's news that the leaf she had handed over upon her return was simply one from a rowan tree. Nothing more.

Questions.

Hoping desperately Bernard's warning was wrong.

The article's final section had been all about their arrival in Hokkaido. Six massively expensive tenders pulling into the harbor of Wakkanai. Docking at quayside between two fishing vessels. Uniformed customs officers had stood outside the main building, smoking cigarettes and laughing over something. Paying them no mind whatsoever.

Almost like they were invisible.

When they arrived at Chitose Airport, Val asked everyone for their names and addresses, explained she was writing an article, and was hoping she might call later and follow up . . .

She did not even need to finish her wind-up. They passed around her notebook. Giving her phone numbers, addresses, emails, the works.

Val left their two guides for last. Iris watched, smiling, as Bernard wrote out his details. When it was her turn, Iris asked, 'You've kept some of the leaves for yourself?'

When she nodded, Bernard said, 'Call me when you're ready.'
'Ready for what?'
Iris laughed. 'That is an *excellent* question.'
Val shouldered her pack and headed out. Thinking that she had her fill of enigmas.

FOURTEEN

When the article was done, Val opened a bottle of Meursault she had been saving for a special occasion. Poured herself a glass and reread. Made a few alterations. Drank a second glass. A third with her stir-fry lunch.

Then she placed the call.

Bernard answered on the first ring. 'Well, hello, stranger.'

'I'm not ready. I'll never be ready. But I want to do this.'

'Great. Shall I come over?'

'You're in Annapolis?'

'Around the corner from your place. Holiday Inn, room 321.'

'OK, that's spooky.'

'Where else should I be?'

'You're here . . . For me?'

He was smiling. She was sure of it. 'My place or yours?'

Val arranged to meet him in a coffee shop midway between her building and old town. It mildly shook her to realize Bernard knew where she lived, and he'd been sitting nearby, waiting. Like a stalker. Only with manners.

The sunlight seemed alien. The street she walked every day, the shops she'd visited hundreds of times, all of it belonged to a different world, someone else's life. Val often felt like this, coming back from a hard assignment. She wanted to tell herself this was the same. But she wasn't in the mood to lie.

She arrived twenty minutes early and chose a table by the rear wall, a corner spot she often used when working on sensitive documents or interviewing a difficult source. She could see everyone, yet remain partially hidden by the barista's counter. She placed her order and opened her laptop, but the words just swam in a jumbled mess. Ten minutes later, she emailed the article to her favorite researcher and requested a FaceTime hookup.

Richie Bond was a genius when it came to hidden online resources. He was also a chameleon. Richie was lean and precise and dressed like a Brooks Brothers ad, ironed shirts and khakis and loafers, the works. He wore round little tortoiseshell glasses and kept his hair trimmed. But all this was a mask. Richie Bond was a merry jester, a crypto freak, a tunnel rat who loved nothing more than strolling the internet's dark ways and stealing whatever caught his fancy.

She settled the pods in her ears and waited for the link. When his face appeared, Richie greeted her with, 'Your license plate ID request really got the bugs swarming.'

'Sorry.'

'Don't apologize. I love watching the feds chase their tails.'

In his previous existence, Richie Bond had been a tax accountant with Ernst and Young. Married, three kids, nice house in the Bethesda 'burbs, his and hers Lexus. Then his wife had decided she didn't love him anymore, and the kids were a mess, and Richie found himself alone and bereft at forty. There wasn't any reason he could see to stay on the straight and narrow. So he turned what had previously been a sideline passion, a hobby with addictive potential, into a new profession. Val had been one of his clients in the tax world, and an almost friend. He had mentioned his love of research one night while going over her annual return. She had been desperate for someone she could trust with the ultra-secret. Somebody who could hunt down what she was incapable of finding herself.

He still did her taxes. He had resigned from the firm, but kept a select few clients as a smokescreen. The semi-retired guy living small. Hah.

Richie told her, 'The article you sent me wasn't encrypted.'

'I want you to read it. Tell me if I'm missing anything.'

Today's shirt was pale bone with narrow pink stripes. Button-down collar. 'This is unexpected.'

'What you have is so totally new it still feels raw. Nine days ago, I didn't even know this thing existed.'

'What thing are we talking about?'

She nodded. 'That is the question I'm chasing.'

Richie examined her. The bland tax accountant with the level gaze. 'Are you in danger?'

'I have no idea. But you'll see when you read, the CIA and the White House are involved.'

'You've agreed to play their tethered goat.' It was not a question.

'Maybe.' She breathed around the prospect. 'Probably.'

'Val, is it worth it?'

'I wish I knew.' She worked the keys. 'My primary contact is a man named Carlton Riffkind. Formerly a K Street lobbyist. Currently a behind-the-scenes mover and shaker. He's an almost friend. His contact details are on the e-mail I've just sent. If I go missing, contact him.'

'Val, no story is worth getting fried.'

She wasn't sure she agreed. But there was no sense in trying to decide on that now. 'I'm sending you a massive file. Almost three hours of video. Ready?'

'Go ahead.'

'Read the article first. Then watch the video. I need you to reduce the footage to something manageable. Fifteen minutes, max twenty. Get in touch when you're ready.'

'And if the wolves catch you in the meantime?'

'Attached to the email with Carlton's contact details is a list of all the editors I've worked with over the past six years. Magazines first, then book publishers. Send both files to them. If they don't move on it, get the article and the video online as fast as you can. And do so anonymously.'

'Val—'

Bernard stepped through the coffee shop's doorway, saw her, and smiled. Val said, 'I have to go.'

FIFTEEN

B ernard refused her offer of a coffee. He seated himself across from her, his back to the room. And waited.

Val decided to give it to him straight. Actually, what happened was, while closing her laptop and watching him cross the room, she accepted there was no alternative. She had no lever that might work with him. No goad. The man was too . . . well, enclosed was the word she had used in the article to describe both him and Iris. Bernard was so comfortable with his calm distance, it seemed to her that nothing would shift him. Possibly not even death. Which only added to her fears.

'I'm going to do this. Don't get me wrong. But I'm terrified.'

'I would be too, in your situation. Definitely.'

She liked his accent. It sounded stronger here, surrounded by simple American twang. The French Caribbean overlaid with a London British smoothness. 'What exactly makes my situation so different from yours? I mean, back when you took the plunge.'

'I know what you mean.' He settled, hooked his hands around his right knee. Utterly relaxed. 'Think back to when you stood at the clearing's periphery.'

'By the glass trees. What were they, by the way?'

'That's not relevant to this moment. It's important we focus on how you felt.'

She accepted because she was already involved in the memory. The sensation was nowhere near as strong as that night, but potent just the same. 'There was a draw. From the tree. Or whatever it was.'

'Good, very good. That makes our work easier. I was concerned . . .'

'What?'

'That you might have just observed. Without the internal effect of being there.'

'No, I definitely felt something.' Then she caught it. 'What, my being there and not participating was some kind of first?'

'As far as we know.'

'Like, the unwelcome outsider?'

'Outsider, yes, though I dislike the word. Unwelcome, definitely not.' He dropped his foot to the floor, leaned forward. 'We need you, Val. Desperately.'

'Who is this "we"?'

'Again with the questions I can't answer until, you know.'

'I take the plunge. Jump over the cliff. Onto the rocks below.'

'No rocks. But the cliff part . . .' He nodded slowly. His waxlike mask and the secretive smile were both gone now. 'If I was in your position, I would definitely call this a high dive.'

'Back to my question. When you heard I'd felt something, you looked, I don't know. Relieved.'

'I am. Definitely.'

'Why?'

'Everyone who's made the journey—'

'Except for me.'

'Except for you, correct. They've felt this draw for days. Weeks. However long it took before they accepted they needed to take this trip. No matter how illogical it might seem. If you hadn't experienced any connection beyond the visual, I don't know what I would have done. What I *could* have done.'

'What about you?'

'I heard about it from a colleague. Afterwards it came to me as a waking image.' He turned slightly, ten degrees, maybe less. Far enough to focus on the wall behind her, and view the past. 'I began seeing the tree at odd moments of the day. I was entering into a crucial segment of lab work on my doctoral thesis. Timing was a vital component of my analysis. Even so, this drew me away. Unlike anything I'd ever experienced. I started calling them events. So powerful I was literally blinded to my lab, the work, the timing issue, everything.'

'Like a hallucination.'

'Yes. And no. This was truly a separate reality. No drug-like effects. I simply entered the clearing. *I was there.*'

'How long did these events last?'

'A minute. Ninety seconds tops. But afterwards . . .'

She breathed the words around her thumping heart. Tight punches of air. Wishing it was just from running another journalistic marathon. 'The draw.'

'Just like you felt. I hope.'

'That's the issue, isn't it. What exactly did I experience? What is the draw?'

'If there are words to describe it,' Bernard replied, 'I have not learned them.'

'I dreamed about it. The tree. Last night. When I woke up . . .'

'Tell me, Val.'

'I was afraid I had left it too late.'

He nodded slowly. 'That must have been hard.'

'And here you are. Lucky me.' When Bernard's only response was his customary smile, she pressed, 'Why did you come?'

'I told you, Val. Your help is crucial. The professional observer. The woman with a voice to the world. As to everything else you want to know, we're back to the same old circular issue. There's only one way to answer. One way for you to understand.'

She sat there. Puffing hard. Tempted to run. Flee. Never look back.

Bernard asked softly, 'Ready?'

'No. Not now. Not ever.'

He rose to his feet. Asked again. 'Ready?'

SIXTEEN

Agnes hated how she was forced to go in blind.

Avri Rowe, White House Chief of Staff, was her boss's boss's boss. She had met the man twice, as in, shaken his hand in events where he greeted the troops. Spoken at three conferences Rowe had attended. Rowe had spent most of the time typing into his phone. Glancing up at certain points, but never fully paying attention. Which meant Agnes had no read on the guy. Nor any idea why he had called for this meeting.

Or why it was taking place here. In the headquarters of Naval Intelligence. Suitland, Maryland. Conference room of the RADM, the rear admiral and commander. Agnes had served in NavIntel for eleven years. Left there for the CIA. Never looked back. Until now.

Grey Mathers was the only other person in the room. Agnes had assumed this mystery meeting was all about the agenda she still carried on her own. Almost. Grey was seated to her right, his chair pushed slightly away from the table. Leaving her alone and exposed.

Avri Rowe was a bullish man with a legendary short temper. She had heard he also possessed a terrifying bark. Which was nothing compared to his bite. 'You have thirty seconds to tell me why this administration should be concerned about whatever is going on in Russia.'

'Sir, you've seen the video?'

'Affirmative. Twenty seconds.'

'It's no longer in Russia, sir. The tree or whatever it was is *gone*. We have to assume it is now a global event. The participants we've been able to identify who were present with Ms Garnier came from eleven different nations.'

Rowe was former army, came out a bird colonel. Two tours in Afghanistan. Switched to the largest defense contractor. Resigned from their board to take his current position. His loyalty to the president was total. 'What would you say is the actual threat level?'

'That's just it, sir. We have no idea. And the longer I'm kept on this leash, the further this *potential* threat might spread.'

'Your current team is . . .'

'What you see. Agent Mathers, myself, one other agent, and two low-level researchers.'

'There is no way we can expand beyond very tight limits. You understand?'

Beside her, Grey's chair squeaked as he shifted. Agnes turned just far enough to freeze him before he voiced his objection. 'Roger that, sir.'

Rowe shot Grey a look of his own. 'Tight limits. One chance to show this is real. Go.'

'The only solid link we have is the journalist.'

'Garnier. The lady Vice President Dale has ordered you not to bring in.'

The fact that the President's Chief of Staff knew of this meeting was good for a highly charged zing. 'Sir, the VP said nothing about people we might identify through her. I suggest we put Garnier under full surveillance. Have a team ready to move the instant she joins a group involved in whatever this is. Bring them all in for interrogation. Except her.'

Rowe gave that a full twenty seconds. Then, 'Your team remains as it currently stands.'

'Sir—'

'Hear me out. Focus exclusively on Garnier.' He took pad and pen from his jacket, wrote swiftly, tore out the page. 'Contact this source. Order whatever electronic surveillance you require.'

She slid the page over, saw a Gmail address of letters and numbers. And a phone number. 'I'm not sure I understand.'

'You don't need to. How long do you require to set up an encrypted feed?'

Grey spoke for the first time. 'Soon as we leave this meeting, it's done.'

'Shoot them the link. Order whatever you think is necessary, right up to satellite reads and drones.' Rowe tapped the page with one stubby finger. 'My private line. The instant you obtain hard intel, you come to me. No one else.'

'Understood, but sir, one request.'

'Go.'

'Carlton Riffkind. I'm certain he knows more than he's saying.'

'You may be right. But in order to move on someone of his standing, what do we need?'

'Concrete, verifiable evidence. Roger that.'

'The very moment you uncover something I can use, you come straight to me.' Rowe stood and started for the door. 'You have one chance to make it work.'

SEVENTEEN

In the end, they returned to her apartment.

He offered his hotel room, then when she blanched he said they could take his car, find a quiet spot—

'It's OK.'

They needed privacy. He had said it twice before. Just in case she . . .

Val put it into strict medical parlance. 'In case I bug out.'

As they walked up the cobblestone street, Val decided having the man in her apartment wasn't such a big deal. After all, Bernard had seen them safely out of Russia. His most dubious act thus far had been to hand her a wad of rubles.

Her building was a post-colonial warehouse, probably once used for shipments of Maryland tobacco and cotton. Thirty-five years ago it had been refashioned into six high-ceilinged condominiums. The rooms were large by contemporary standards, and the builders had sealed and polished the original brick walls and massive ceiling beams. The floors were broad planks, painstakingly restored and sealed in place with square-headed, hand-forged iron nails. Val's furniture had been carefully selected. There were a lot of empty spaces, because she bought when she could afford another item that she truly loved. Most were modern renditions of Jacobean and colonial originals, but handcrafted by artisans. They, like the apartment, had cost a bomb.

Bernard took his time, appreciating everything. 'This is not what I expected.'

'You were after goth and edgy, perhaps?'

'Contemporary. Perhaps a bit more flash.' He nodded over the walnut dining table. 'It suits you, Val.'

'Where do you want to do this?'

'It's your home. Your move. Where will you be most comfortable?'

'That word, comfort.' She heard the slight jump she was adding to each word. Fear, pure and simple. 'It has no place in this scenario.'

'Where will you be least likely to do a freak on me?' He smiled at her. 'Did I say that right? Do a freak?'

'Your English is nearly perfect, and you're enjoying this.'

'Well of course I am. I've been sitting in a bland and sterile hotel room, waiting for your call. Not knowing if it would happen.' His smile was gone now, but not the spark to his gaze. 'This is a first. A major event. I'm genuinely excited.'

Hearing that calmed her. A little. 'How about the sofa?'

'Sofa it is. I suggest we use one of the leaves you took.'

She remained standing by the kitchen counter. 'Aren't you the least bit concerned I gave one of them to the CIA?'

Bernard's response was to walk over, seat himself, and pat the cushion beside him. 'Delaying tactics don't take us where we want to go, Val.'

She entered the kitchen, opened the drawer by the fridge, and pulled out the plastic baggie holding the fifteen leaves she had kept. She carried it over to the sofa, her hands shaking like, well, a leaf.

Bernard pushed back a trifle, keeping his distance. 'Pick one.'

She had trouble taking hold and drawing it out.

'Now close your eyes. Think back to when you were standing in the clearing.'

Her terrified mind held to a firework display of fragmented impressions. She couldn't think of anything. Her name . . . Camilla? Mortitia?

When it happened.

She felt *the draw*.

Her heart held to its frantic drumbeat. Her hands still trembled. But her mind . . .

Stilled.

She was silenced by the sudden intensity. It was not calm. And it was not *out there*. She was not held by some external force. This was *hers*. Val had no idea how she could be so certain of anything. Just the same, she knew with utter conviction that the sensation was not just some fleeting emotion.

By taking this first step, she had arrived at a point which had escaped her for basically her entire life. She could still her mind. Without the crutch of drugs or hour-long dance sessions or sex or whatever. What she experienced was stronger than all of that. Including the frantic beat of fear. Then . . .

She was back at the tree.

This was not some dream that whispered to her. Not a potent memory. *She was there.*

She knew this for certain, the journalist at work even now. She noticed something she had missed before, lost to the entirety of all those new sensations.

She smelled a unique fragrance of forest and raw earth and wild northern blossoms. And the sea. The wind in her face carried a salty Arctic tang.

And there before her, the tree. Grand and burnished and waiting.

'Open your eyes, Val.' Only now Bernard's voice had captured a trace of her own unsteadiness. 'Go ahead. Look.'

The leaf was gone.

In its place was a small, weightless bundle, shimmering in the palm of her hand.

Bernard asked once more, 'Ready?'

She nodded. Yes. And for the first time, she was.

Sure, there was that tiny whisper of fearful warning, like the hiss of a kettle boiling in a different room. No louder than before she snorted another line or took a final hit off the bong, long after she had left her limit in the night's rearview mirror.

This was the same. Only different.

Her whispering, shrieking fear was twofold.

Losing control. Always a big issue with her.

And facing the unknown. Which both terrified and beckoned.

The story of her life.

'Place it wherever you like,' Bernard said. 'It invited you. Now you do the same.'

She hesitated, but not because she fought the action. Instead, she drew out the exquisite moment. She was *committed.*

Doing like Iris, applying the thread to her head and fashioning the crown, seemed over the top. Too much of the earth-mother-queen vibe. And around the wrist seemed, well, lame.

She lifted the brilliant bundle and touched the space over her heart.

EIGHTEEN

Val felt . . .

Nothing.

A faint tingling started in her head and descended to her neck. More than likely, though, it was the result of her system being drenched in adrenaline and fear.

She dropped the hand hovering above her heart. Turned to the smiling Bernard. Hated to disappoint him. Hating to have failed.

Then she sensed . . .

Others.

There was a sudden shift in the room's atmosphere. A silent, secret wind. Opening an unseen door. Revealing . . .

She was connected. People were there with her. And Bernard. With them both.

These were not strangers. The fact that she didn't know them and might never even meet, at least physically, was not the key factor at work here.

She. Was. Not. Alone.

The realization of being linked left her wanting to weep.

There was no pressure to these connections. No pushing at her. No reading of her mind. No crowding into her existence. Just the same, she knew the word for what she was sensing.

Telepathy.

She said, 'They've got it all wrong.'

Bernard nodded. 'It was never about reading thoughts. Why on earth would I want to hear the clutter inside your head? Listening to mine is bad enough.'

'This is . . . wild.'

'And it's only starting. You know how both Iris and I went back to the tree? We were seeking to bond at a deeper level.'

'OK, so . . .'

'Normally we let newcomers settle in for a couple of months. But we don't have time, Val. Not with you. There's an issue we need your help with. It's not time-sensitive. It's time-*crucial*.'

She got up. Walked away from him. And in so doing, the physical movement gave her the strength to push away the people.

And just like that, they were gone. The door was closed. *Her* door.

No pressure to hold on. No invasion of her space.

Unless she wanted.

'I could use a tea. You?'

'Thank you, tea would be nice.'

She busied her hands. Matcha green. Rough ceramic mugs. 'You like honey?'

'Sure.'

She was glad he could be patient despite the urgency. She felt it now. A faint trembling to the air, a vibratory pattern that spelled out the single word, *alarm*. Even so, she needed a moment, and Bernard knew it, and he was waiting with her.

So she made the tea and poured two mugs and added honey to both and walked back over. Seated herself. Sipped. Shut her eyes.

And opened the door again.

This time it was clearer. People in three different groups. Actually, she decided *set* worked better. One set was Bernard. The other was a doctor. Or monitor. Someone responsible for keeping record of who was . . .

The word was there waiting for her. *Alert.*

That was how they defined this listening state. Being alert.

She liked that. She liked it a lot.

And the third group. They were the ones who needed her . . .

She jerked so hard she spilled the hot tea on her hand.

'Steady, now.' Bernard took a handkerchief from his pocket, dabbed her hand. 'Easy does it.'

She opened her eyes. Sipped. Tried again.

The group consisted of twenty-six people. All scientists of one ilk or another.

Physicists. Theoretical and applied. Engineers, mostly electrical, though two focused on nuclear. Several mathematicians.

They were *desperate*. All of them. Waiting for *her* to help establish a new compass heading.

'Good,' Bernard said softly. 'Very good.'

She started to say she was ready to go. Right then and there. Do what she could to help them.

When suddenly . . .

She looked at Bernard. Eyes so wide it felt like her brows touched her hairline. Mouth a circle. Because . . .

Bernard asked, 'What?'

'I need to ask somebody else to join us.'

He leaned back. Utterly flummoxed. 'Are you sure?'

'Bernard, his presence is absolutely critical. Life or death.'

He covered his mouth with the hand not holding his mug. His shoulders trembled.

Val realized he was laughing. 'What?'

'The night after we left the island. Iris said you were going to be a huge help.'

'Are you sure Iris was talking about me? I'm only asking because her reaction at the tree wasn't all that positive.'

'Just the same. Iris said you were going to astonish us all. She insisted I come.'

'Iris told you to come to Annapolis?'

'I didn't want to. I thought it was a waste of time. I needed to restart my research, and you seemed so set on your isolated course.' Bernard smiled. 'Iris loves being right.'

'Back to the matter at hand. Can I contact this person?'

'It's fine by me. But we need to make sure it's all right with the others.'

'So what do I do?'

'Is it a man or woman?'

'Man.'

'Have you two had a relationship?'

'Not like you're meaning. But I've known him a long time.'

'Speak his name. Try to bring an image of him to mind. Not so much how he looks, you understand?'

'How he is to me. Down deep.'

'Where it matters,' Bernard confirmed. 'Ready?'

'Yes.' She closed her eyes. Found herself confronting any number of watchers. She turned from them, not shutting the internal portal. Just focusing elsewhere and inviting them along for the ride. When she was ready, she began, 'His name is Carlton Riffkind . . .'

NINETEEN

That afternoon at half past five, Carlton was in his private study, seated in his Eames chair, enjoying a first glass of Cardhu Gold, his absolute favorite single-malt whisky. Through his closed door he could hear two women talking. His wife Marina and daughter Alexi. His daughter was twenty-eight and recently divorced, back living with them, her and their only grand-baby, Mindy. The little baby girl so resembled Alexi at that age, it brought tears to his eyes. Truth be told, he was glad the two had moved back home. And not just because he and his wife both thought Alexi's soon-to-be ex was a louse. When they first started hearing hints that things were not well on the home front, Carlton had sent his private investigator out to have a look-see. The evidence was in a file in his bottom drawer now. Video, stills, voice. Made for quite a putrid viewing. The ex did not know it yet. But if he even hinted at giving them trouble, he'd discover soon enough that his goose was crispy fried.

The little one, Mindy, was a sweetheart. And having Alexi and the eleven-month baby girl back under their roof had taken years off his wife. Decades. Marina had always been active in her own profession, a strong voice for families and special-needs education with multiple administrations. But Mindy and Alexi had added a genuine and much-needed spark to their home and their lives.

The home study was Carlton's ultra-private space. No cleaner entered. He hoovered and dusted himself, when it suited. It was all the man cave he had ever needed. If a meeting at home was required, he used the dining room. This was his space, and his alone.

He had requested and been given the CIA's growing file on Valentina Garnier. He skimmed the pages as he lowered the level of his glass. He slipped the large photographs to one side, then spread them out so she looked up at him from a variety of angles.

He had always liked Val. Her work and the professional manner she maintained, no matter what the level of stress and pressure, had impressed Carlton. Reading the details of how she became the lady she was only added spice to the curry. Agnes and her focus on Val's use of the odd drug was absurd. The lady deserved her releases. Spoken by a man with a cut-crystal glass of single malt in his hand.

Valentina was not a traditional sort of beauty. Too edgy. Too in-your-face. Too intelligent. A very sharp and perceptive woman, who had fought off a truly awful childhood and become a genuine success. Abuse of the heart might not leave the same sort of visible scars, but the impact could be just as searing. He thought he could see a bit of that in her gaze, even now. Like a pair of opals that had been wrapped in the blanket of time, and smashed with an uncaring hammer.

She did not look American. There was a refined French nature to her dark hair, skin, high cheekbones, full lips. If Carlton had been a younger man and single, well . . . No need to dwell on that.

Which was when the doorbell rang.

Something about the manner of his wife's voice had him gathering up the photos and stowing the file in his top drawer before Marina knocked and opened and said, 'Carlton, there's a young lady here. She says it is urgent.'

He then heard Val's voice call from the foyer, 'Life or death, Carlton. For real.'

TWENTY

They left for Reagan National Airport twenty-seven minutes later. Carlton was less than satisfied with Val's responses to his questions. And the microbiologist from Martinique by way of London, Bernard, had not spoken at all. Just the same, Carlton had come along for the ride. Val had not actually promised answers. Instead, she had said if he wanted to fully understand what was happening, he needed to take this first step. Nothing more.

They passed through the private air terminal in record time. A uniformed pilot was there in the lobby; how he had been alerted was anyone's guess. No one in Carlton's company had made any advance call. The pilot led them through a perfunctory TSA inspection and guided them over to a Lear whose engines were already revving. Nine minutes later, they were aloft.

Three others were on the plane. Two women, one man. Early thirties, highly intelligent, scruffy, dressed like postdocs right the world around. The young man was Oriental, the ladies both Anglo. All were clearly stressed. Worried. Afraid. They watched in silence as Carlton seated himself across the aisle, with Val and Bernard facing him.

They flew north by west, the dimming sunlight making a spectacle of their passage over Washington's sprawl. Carlton accepted their offer of a coffee and sandwich. The copilot put a fresh pot on to brew and unwrapped a silver Salver of crustless sandwiches. He served them all, said their flight time was fifty-three minutes, and retreated to the cockpit. Carlton's cup and plate were both Limoges, gold-rimmed. Linen napkin. One sandwich was smoked salmon with cucumber, the other rare roast beef with sprouts and whole-grain mustard. The coffee was delicious.

'All right,' he said. 'I'm listening.'

Their spokesperson was a woman seated at a forty-five-degree angle from Carlton, across the aisle, dark-haired and heavyset and tight, almost angry. 'We need your promise you won't discuss what we're about to disclose with anyone outside this group. Unless we give a green light. Which will only be offered on a case-by-case basis.'

Carlton took another of the roast beef sandwiches. There was no rush, as far as he was concerned. He addressed Val, 'Does this mean you wish to hire me as a consultant?'

Her tone was unequivocal. 'Absolutely.'

The dark-haired woman snorted softly. 'That is yet to be determined.'

Bernard was seated next to the window, with Val between him and the aisle. The man had still not spoken. Bernard observed Val with what Carlton thought was an approving smile.

Carlton asked, 'Can you afford me?'

'You see how we're traveling,' Val replied. 'Payment is not the issue.'

'Correction. Payment is always an issue. But it's nice to hear you say that. Next question. Does this have any connection to the vice president's daughter?'

The dark-haired woman snapped, 'That's none of your concern.'

'Correction, Ms . . . I'm sorry. Might I ask your name?'

'Larkins. And it's Doctor.'

'Dr Larkins, you are clearly an expert at something. It so happens I am as well. And one reason for my having achieved this level of success is the code by which I operate. These rules may not be as rigid as the boundaries to your own profession. But they are, for me, at least, unbreakable.'

She glared at Val. 'This is going nowhere.'

'Let him finish.' Val seemed as unfazed by the woman's ire as Bernard.

'And he's taking too long.'

'Go on, Carlton. You were saying?'

'I never accept a new client when there is the slightest whiff of conflict with another. Which means there must be an absolute acceptance of harmony with my current work for Vice President Dale and his family. And such harmony can only be achieved through total transparency.'

'We agree,' Val said.

Larkins leaned forward. 'Really, Bernard? Really?'

Carlton went on, 'What is more, Terrance Dale happens to be a close personal friend. If this can help him and his wife come to terms with what has happened to his daughter, he *must* know. And if I agree to be part of whatever is going on, he *will* know.'

Val astonished him then. And in a lifetime of scaling the political heights and surviving any number of bruising battles, Carlton had come to think very little could still manage to surprise him.

This, however, knocked him to next week.

Val turned to the woman and said, 'We need him also.'

Dr Larkins was still leaning forward, doing her best to ignore Val entirely. 'She's already said that! Bernard, look at me! This is the exact opposite . . .' She stopped because Val planted an open hand in her face. '*What?*'

'Not Carlton,' Val said, utterly cool with it all. 'The vice president. He must be involved.'

For the first time since boarding the flight, Bernard became fully engaged. 'Are you sure about that?'

'I am. Yes.'

His response was another astonishment. He gripped Val's hand. Tightly. Then said, 'Elizabeth.'

The scientist crossed her arms. 'No.'

'Now, Elizabeth.'

'This is taking us *nowhere*.' Larkins reached across the aisle. Hesitated, hovering. Then planted her hand atop Bernard's.

Bernard said, 'Chakkan, Sandra, join us.'

The Oriental gentleman and the woman seated next to Larkins had to rise to their feet. Which they did. And planted their hands on top of the other three.

Ten seconds later, it was over.

Whatever it was.

Chakkan and Sandra retook their seats. Larkins settled back, utterly flummoxed. Confused. Her fear no longer masked by anger. 'I still don't . . .'

'Elizabeth. Enough.' Bernard asked Val, 'What do you propose?'

'I see one way forward. Carlton must be involved. And through him, the VP.'

The woman named Sandra asked, 'What if he says no?'

'If he signs on, great. We'll work out the hows and whens after. If not . . .' She shrugged. 'I have no idea. Hopefully we'll see an alternative.'

Bernard corrected, '*You* will see.'

Larkins asked Bernard, 'You trust her this much?'

Chakkan spoke for the first time. 'You've seen it. Same as me. Same as all of us.'

When they all went silent, Carlton demanded, 'Seen what?'

Val smiled. 'It's kind of hard to explain.'

TWENTY-ONE

I mmediately following her meeting with Avri Rowe, Agnes requisitioned a basement office in some nondescript federal structure off M Street. The last thing she wanted or needed was to try and run this op from the fishbowl environment of CIA head-quarters in Langley.

Homeland held leases on any number of such facilities, a relic from the post-Covid period when their new campus across the river in Virginia was not yet operational. The A/C barely worked, the walls glistened with damp, and the carpet was frayed and blackened around the edges. Agnes could have cared less. She had a secure fiber-optic connection to her new surveillance team, and there was more than enough room for Grey, her second agent, and the two researchers.

She also had a new off-the-books sat phone. She had long suspected the NSA monitored all conversations on her designated CIA device. She used her new phone to make this call.

The president's chief of staff answered with his customary bark. 'Who is this?'

'Agnes Pendalon, sir.'

'I don't have either time or interest in any preliminary updates.'

'Sir, I think we may have our window of opportunity.'

'What, already?'

'It appears that way.'

'In that case, you may have a full minute of my time. Go.'

'Carlton Riffkind and Valentina Garnier just boarded a private jet at Reagan National. Already on board are three scientists, two from MIT and one from the University of Pennsylvania. All three are on our suspect list.'

'What does this list of yours signify?'

'These are the individuals and families we believe traveled to Russia.'

A momentary silence, then, 'Destination?'

'The flight plan shows Williamsport Municipal Airport.'

'Where is that?'

'Western Pennsylvania.'

'Hold one.'

Agnes' attention was drawn to her normally stoic aide. Grey bounced in his seat, face taut, eyes shining with the same electric tension Agnes felt. When she caught his gaze, all he said was, 'Finally.'

Avri Rowe chose that moment to come back on. 'How fast can you get to Andrews Air Force Base?'

Her two agents were already up and moving. 'Thirty minutes. Less.'

'A team will be ready to board upon your arrival. They operate under your command. Good hunting.'

TWENTY-TWO

They landed in the last glimmering blades of summer dusk. The Williamsport Municipal Airport serviced towns throughout the lovely Pennsylvania hill country. The jet taxied away from the small terminal and stopped by a dome-shaped hangar. Two Honda people-carriers were parked beneath the exterior lights. Soon as Elizabeth Larkins descended the jet's stairs, a trio of young people in lab coats rushed over, holding up tablets and jabbering. She joined them in the first vehicle, and they sped jabbering.

Sandra pointed the rest of them toward the second vehicle and slipped behind the wheel. Carlton allowed himself to be guided into the second seat, and Val joined him. Bernard took the front passenger seat, and the Oriental man slipped into the back.

As they pulled through the perimeter fence, Carlton asked, 'Where are we going?'

'Mostly north, a little west,' Bernard replied. 'Half an hour tops. Just outside the Susquehannock State Forest.'

Carlton paused through two beats, then asked again, 'Where are we going?'

Chakkan laughed softly.

Bernard turned in his seat. 'Patience.'

Carlton asked the young man, 'Am I correct in assuming you are also a specialist at something, Dr Chakkan?'

'Chakkan is my first name, Mr Riffkind. Don't bother with my last. It has seventeen syllables. My mother can't pronounce it. She says it is the second worse burden she took on when she married my father.'

'Where are you from?'

'Thailand.'

'And you're here because . . .'

'I was doing postdoc research at MIT. Electrical engineering.'

Their driver said, 'You still are.'

'We'll see.'

'Don't give me that,' Sandra replied. 'Don't you dare.'

Carlton leaned toward the driver and asked, 'Sandra, you are . . .'

'First names are good enough, sir. UPenn. Professor of higher math.'

'Please, everyone, call me Carlton.' He studied the silhouettes of forest closing in to either side of the two-lane road. 'Well, at least I don't have to listen to the good Dr Larkins moan for the next thirty minutes.'

'She wasn't moaning,' Chakkan said. 'She was venting.'

Sandra said, 'She does that a lot. Vent.'

'Tell me.'

Carlton said, 'I take it whatever's happened to you folks, it doesn't have you holding hands and singing kumbaya.'

'Kumbaya,' Chakkan said. 'Was that on the Beatles' White album?'

Sandra said, 'I'll pay a hundred bucks to anyone who asks Dr Larkins to sing that.'

'Not a chance,' Chakkan replied. 'You think she vented on the plane. Hah.'

'OK, a thousand dollars.'

Val offered, 'I'll do it.'

'No, you won't.' This from Bernard. 'Apparently we need you intact.'

'She doesn't look that tough. Besides, I've stripped naked and danced on a table for half that. Not my finest hour, I admit. But a thousand bucks is a thousand bucks.'

That silenced the van, until Chakkan said, 'I've got . . . Four and change. Who's with me?'

Carlton winked at Val. 'I believe I have some spare cash on me.'

'No stripping,' Bernard said. 'No kumbaya. No dancing.'

'You sound like my mother,' Chakkan replied.

Sandra flashed a smile. 'Aw, Bernie. And here I thought you were a fun-loving cutie pie.'

'Don't call me that.'

'What, cutie pie?'

'My name is Bernard. Dr Severant to you lot.'

Sandra turned back to the road. 'Cutie pie.'

And just like that, Carlton was simply part of the crew. Comfortable enough to face Val and say, 'You did it, didn't you? That thing with the leaf.'

'Of course I did.'

He mentally fumbled his way through a dozen questions. A hundred. Settled on, 'But when I saw you in your apartment . . .'

'No. Not at that point.'

'I don't understand. The tree is *gone*. And the leaves are just that. Unless you passed along a fake to the CIA.'

'No, it was real. We'll get to that. I promise.'

'That's all you're giving me?'

'No, Carlton. But just now, there's something much more important—'

'I need a little, Val. Help me understand enough to be comfortable with this mystery trip.'

Chakkan said, 'Mystery is right.'

'Quiet in the ranks,' Bernard said.

'He thinks he's got mystery now—'

'Chakkan.' This from Sandra. 'Apply the sock.'

When the van went quiet, Carlton said, 'Please.'

She turned so that they were knee to knee. 'I'm still an investigative journalist. That hasn't changed.'

'Don't give me some "nothing's changed" fable. Don't you dare.'

'I'm not saying it's all the same. There is definitely an enhancement. But it's based on me. Who I was, that's who I am.' She gave him a chance to speak, then went on, 'We all change. All the time. Every seven years, all the cells in our body are different. But we remain the same. At the core level, of consciousness or spirit or whatever you want to call it. Yes, I have been enhanced. But my purpose, my role, it's the same. I investigate. Uncover the unseen. Reveal the hidden. Follow the logical pattern of evidence.'

Carlton realized Bernard had turned in his seat and was watching her. Eyes gleaming. Carlton looked back and saw Chakkan had switched positions, arms crossed on the seat-back, chin resting on his wrists, watching. Chakkan offered, 'Enhancement. I love it.'

Sandra asked, 'How long since she . . .'

'Nine hours and counting,' Bernard said.

'Wow.'

'Amazing,' Chakkan said.

Carlton asked, 'So this line of evidence, it brings us here?'

'Not us,' Val replied. 'Well, sure, we're all here for a reason. But the line of evidence I followed was directed at your presence. Just you. Specifically.'

'But if I understand this correctly, what we're actually dealing with here are future events,' Carlton said. 'Which means your evidence applied to things that have not yet happened?'

She shrugged. 'I have no idea how to answer that. When I . . .'

'Reach out,' Bernard suggested.

'Connect,' Chakkan said.

She nodded. 'Sooner or later we're going to have to come up with new words.'

'You will,' Chakkan said. 'The writer.'

'Back to my question,' Carlton said.

'In those moments of being connected, I can't tell the difference between the *now* and the *next.*'

Again the van went silent. Then Chakkan said, 'OK. Chills.'

'Iris said Val would prove vital to our projects,' Bernard said. 'Iris loves being right.'

Val glanced forward. 'Projects, plural?'

Chakkan actually laughed. 'What, you thought all we need you for was this little kumbaya in the Pennsylvania hill country?'

Carlton demanded, but softly, 'What exactly is waiting for us up there?'

'The million-dollar question,' Bernard said.

'Billion, more like,' Sandra added.

'Someone. Please.'

'He needs to know,' Bernard said.

'Ahem,' Chakkan said. 'May I?'

Sandra said, 'OK, Dr Thai Exchange Student. The floor is yours.'

'Mr Riffkind, Carlton, what you see here, this gathering, it doesn't simply happen. Today's world is all about specialization. Which is basically another word for division. But what you're about to see is only possible because of our joining together. And no, I'm not just talking about the event itself. This goes much deeper. And the impact is, well, you'll see for yourself in about . . .'

'Twenty minutes,' Sandra said. 'Less.'

'Sandra specializes in higher math and possible links to theoretical physics. The venting Dr Larkins is an astrophysicist and a world-renowned expert on black holes and their relationship to dark energy. All the others you met on the plane and those waiting up ahead, they represent a broad spectrum of cutting-edge science and theoretical physics. Except for me. The good Dr Larkins thinks I'm one step above the plumber called in to fix her sink.'

'Dr Larkins,' Sandra said, 'is first cousin to a loon.'

'A very smart loon,' Bernard said.

'Moving on,' Chakkan said. 'At their basic level, since the discovery of fire and the harnessing of steam, most of man's attempts to exploit power have been *violent*. We create explosions of one kind or another, and then derive a useable portion of energy. A *small* portion. Solar and wind and water power are all steps in the right direction. But still very inefficient. And what we are seeking to do here—'

'What we've done,' Sandra corrected. 'Sixteen times and counting.'

'It requires a huge amount of power. To give you an example, the average nuclear plant produces around one gigawatt. What you're about to witness requires *nineteen gigawatts*.'

'Is this dangerous?' Carlton asked.

'Driving these roads after dark is dangerous,' Sandra said. 'Breathing.'

Chakkan lifted himself higher. 'Who is doing the explaining here?'

'Your pardon, good sir. The floor is yours.'

'According to the lambda-CDM model of cosmology, current estimates are that dark energy represents sixty-eight percent of the total energy in the observable universe. We are tapping into that. And the method for this basically comes down to *harmonizing*. We create an environment where we *invite* the energy into our physical world. It *volunteers* itself to be translated into a form where it can interact with our definable universe.'

Sandra was watching him in her rearview mirror. 'You know, that was actually very good.'

'I'll say,' Val agreed. 'I actually understood. A little. Some.'

'Eyes on the dangerous nighttime road,' Bernard said.

'Sure thing, Dr Bernie.'

Chakkan continued, 'When we arrive, if you ask and maybe even if you don't, the good Dr Larkins will fill your head with terms like dark energy's density—'

'Cosmological constant,' Sandra said. 'Dark matter versus baryonic matter. Give her a chance, she'll go on forever.'

'Scalar fields,' Bernard said. 'I remember hearing that somewhere.'

'Dynamic quantities that vary in time and space,' Sandra said. 'I can scare you up a pillow and blanket if you feel like having a nap.'